I0726686

SO REVEALING

KYLIE GILMORE

Copyright © 2017 by Kylie Gilmore

All rights reserved. No part of this publication may be reproduced, distributed, or transmitted in any form or by any means, including photocopying, recording, or other electronic or mechanical methods, without the prior written permission of the writer, except in the case of brief quotations embodied in critical reviews and certain other noncommercial uses permitted by copyright law.

This is a work of fiction. Names, characters, places, brands, media, and incidents are the product of the author's imagination or are used fictitiously. The author acknowledges the trademarked status and trademark owners of various products referenced in this work of fiction, which have been used without permission. The publication/use of these trademarks are not authorized, associated with, or sponsored by the trademark owners. Any resemblance to actual events, locales, or persons, living or dead, is purely coincidental.

So Revealing: © 2017 by Kylie Gilmore

Cover design by Sweet 'N Spicy Designs

Published by: Extra Fancy Books

ISBN-13: 978-1-942238-28-7

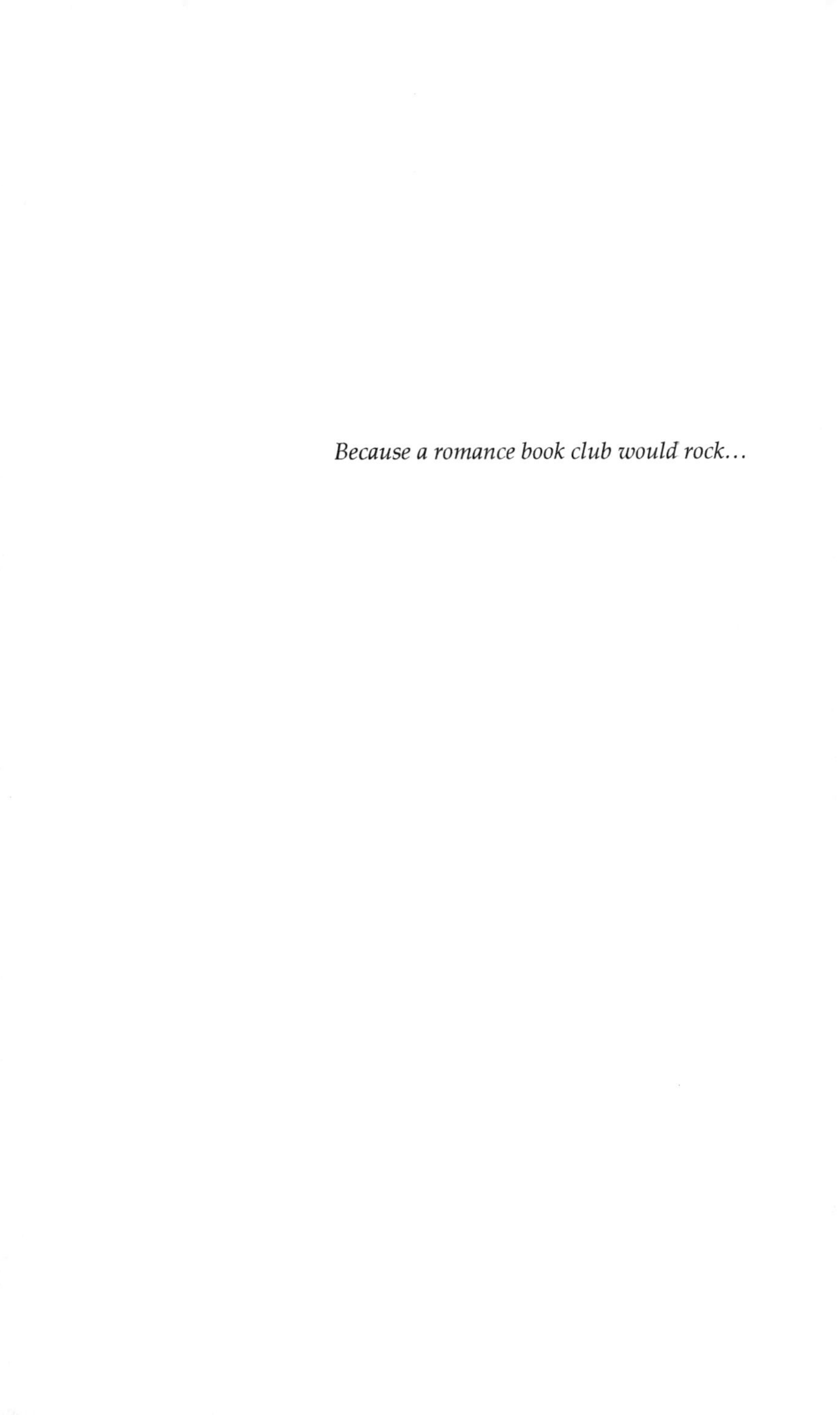

Because a romance book club would rock…

1

———

"How romantic are you?"

Charlotte Vega stifled a laugh at her friend's question aimed at the Campbell brothers and their guy friends sitting further down the bar. Men were *not* romantic. Hailey was on the edge of her seat, eager for any juicy romantic nugget.

No juice. No romantic nugget either.

Charlotte could've saved Hailey a lot of time and frustration tonight if only Hailey had listened. Men liked food, sports, and sex. Romance didn't enter the equation. Exhibit A: the men in question snarfed down brownies and beer, eyes glued to the March Madness college basketball game on the TV mounted over the bar. Charlotte had to admit the men were easy on the eyes—most of them of the tall, dark, and muscular variety. It wasn't a stretch to imagine sex was never far from their minds (once they had their fill of food and sports).

"Scale of one to ten?" Hailey asked, her voice rising in desperation. As Clover Park's one and only wedding planner, Hailey Adams was hell-bent on matchmaking the single women in the Happy Endings Book Club and felt it her mission to better understand single men to do so. She was under the delusion she'd already caused three members to find their special someone.

Charlotte was about to tell Hailey to give up already when God's gift to women swaggered into the bar, wearing a black leather jacket, faded blue jeans, and hiking boots. His dark hair was cropped short; his dark brown eyes crinkled at the corners with a smile that flashed white against the dark shadow of stubble on his square jaw. Of course, he completely ignored her, just like before. He exuberantly greeted the guys —his brothers—with pound-on-the-back bro hugs. Then he stopped to greet some of her friends, kissing Hailey on the cheek, who sat on one side of Charlotte, and ruffling the hair of his sister, Mad, who sat on her other side.

Like Charlotte cared if he ignored her.

"Hi, Charlotte," Ty said casually like he hadn't dissed her big time the last time she saw him. "Long time no see."

"Hello," she said coolly.

Ty settled on the bar stool next to Hailey. Even though there was only one person between them, Charlotte refused to look in that direction. She'd had the unfortunate experience of meeting the arrogant Ty Campbell at his brother's wedding last Christmas. It had been three months and it still bugged her the way Ty purposely asked all of her friends to dance at the wedding reception, even his own damn sister, and not her. Then he'd had the audacity to act like he hadn't been playing a game to gain her attention and get her to ask him. Ha! Charlotte had had enough bad relationships to last a lifetime, from cheaters to liars to men with serious emotional baggage. And she sure as hell didn't play games.

She took a sip of martini and turned to talk to Mad. She waited patiently for Mad to focus, given she was in her fiancé's lap and he was nuzzling her neck.

Ty's deep booming voice was impossible to ignore. "What'd I miss? I'll answer all your questions, sweetheart."

"Thank you," Hailey replied sweetly. "I was asking the guys how romantic they considered themselves on a scale of one to ten."

Charlotte risked a look over.

Ty chose that moment to peel off his leather jacket, revealing a black T-shirt and massive biceps covered in tribal tattoos. Her pulse kicked into high gear at the spectacular arm porn. "On a scale of one to ten," he drawled, his gaze fixed on Hailey, "I'd say ten."

"Ha!" Charlotte blurted. The man had dissed her big time. That was *not* romantic.

Ty's eyes met hers, a small smirk of a smile playing over his lips. "I can turn up the heat when I want to."

"Heat is not the same as romance," Charlotte returned. *Clueless man.*

Ty ignored that. "What else you got, sweetheart?" he asked Hailey.

Hailey beamed, her pale blue eyes shining with adoration. "I must say you're much more cooperative than your brothers and brothers from another mother."

Charlotte stifled a laugh. Hailey was one of those classy refined women who couldn't quite pull off slang. The Campbells had a posse of honorary brothers, guys that had grown up close to the Campbell family.

Hailey tossed her strawberry blonde hair over her shoulder. "Okay, next question. When was the last time you laughed out loud?"

Ty flashed a devilish grin. "With Park on the ride over here when he told me the guys were going to answer your romance questions in exchange for brownies and free beer."

Hailey harrumphed.

Charlotte bit back a smile, not wanting to encourage Ty. The man was incorrigible.

Ty's beer arrived and he took a sip before saying, "Not every guy is in touch with his romantic side like I am. You found that out by now, right?"

So cocky. So full of himself. Charlotte didn't want to listen to another word from this unbearable—

Stop. Don't let him in your head.

Hailey elbowed her and whispered, "Bet you his answer to the outdoor question is much better than the other guys'." That was the only question the guys had answered—to Hailey's shock and dismay—claiming that sex was their favorite outdoor activity. Probably just to mess with Hailey. *Nailed it.*

"I doubt it," Charlotte murmured before draining her martini.

"Favorite outdoor activity?" Hailey asked Ty.

Ty gave Charlotte a wink. "I'd love to tell you that, but I think Josh might throttle me." He smirked at his older brother Josh, the bartender and manager of Garner's Sports Bar & Grill, who was pointedly ignoring the conversation.

Hailey glanced at Josh, who stared back with his deep soulful brown eyes. They had a frenemy thing that had escalated into all-out war. Most recently Hailey had started a rumor that Josh had an affliction that left him impotent. He still didn't know that was the reason he had big tips and little action. Charlotte really hoped she was around for the explosion when he found out. Some said it would be a quick flip between the pair from hate to love. Charlotte suspected they enjoyed being frenemies too much to ever stop.

Hailey leaned close to Ty. "Just whisper it to me."

Ty whispered something, and Hailey gasped. "Did the guys tell you to say that?"

"Did they say the same thing?" Ty asked.

"Yes!" Hailey exclaimed.

Ty threw back his head and laughed. "What can I tell you, probably all guys would say that. Right, Josh?"

Josh grumbled something and shifted to the other side of the bar.

It was like they all read from the same damn playbook.

"Men!" Hailey exclaimed, throwing her hands up. "Sex on the brain. Where is the romance?"

Charlotte rubbed Hailey's back, feeling a little protective of her friend's naivety. This was exactly why she'd given up on men three years ago. All the heartache had led to a lot of emotional eating. She used to be more than a hundred pounds heavier than she was now. She'd gotten herself into a gym, worked with a personal trainer, and was so inspired with the results she became a personal trainer herself. Now she only dated men on her terms—when and where she chose and never for anything serious.

Ty piped up. "You can have both sex and romance."

Charlotte shot him a disbelieving look before comforting Hailey. "Romance doesn't exist in real life. Why do you think we read it in book club? It's a female fantasy."

"You can have both," Ty insisted. "Just because Charlotte never—"

Charlotte glared at him and he shut up. For a moment, anyway.

"Damn, woman," Ty said in what sounded like appreciation, "that's one lethal look you got going on. Bet that keeps men away."

"Shut up," Charlotte snapped.

Hailey turned to Ty. "No, don't shut up. Keep talking. Have you had both romance and, you know, the other?"

"Once," he said in a surprisingly subdued tone. "Turned out she was using me for an intro to a director, who she slept with. Next question." Ty was a stuntman with a lot of movie credits.

Hailey barreled on. "Would you date someone who makes more money than you?"

Ty lifted one massive shoulder up and down. "Depends." He slid Charlotte a sly look. "How much money do you make, Char?"

"That is an extremely rude question," she informed him. And a very strange way of flirting.

Hailey was on a roll. "If you could have dinner with anyone alive or dead, who would it be?"

Ty stood and shifted around Hailey, right up into Charlotte's personal space. God, he smelled good. Woodsy, musk, hint of citrus. He smelled like fresh sex in the outdoors. Oh no!

He smiled down at Charlotte. "I'd like to have dinner with you."

"Are you good with your hands?" Hailey asked, standing close to Ty now, completely oblivious to the fact that Ty was making a move.

But Charlotte was intensely aware, her breath shallow, hot from head to toe. She blinked, trying to formulate a snappy comeback that would give her the distance she needed to breathe normally again. Ty was leaning dangerously close to her. Kissing close.

He suddenly veered and spoke in a husky voice near her ear. "Very good."

Her brain felt foggy. "Huh?"

He straightened. "I'm very good with my hands."

"Great!" Hailey chirped.

"Oh," Charlotte said in a brilliant comeback.

"How do you spend your free time?" Hailey asked.

Ty answered while gazing into Charlotte's eyes. "With Charlotte, I hope. Have dinner with me this weekend?"

"No." Oh, good. Her brain was working again.

Ty's mouth hung open like he'd never been told no before.

"Well!" Hailey exclaimed. "Wow! Okay! Thank you for your honest answers. I'll just step back over here."

She left.

"So, back to dinner," Ty said, leaning his arm on the bar next to her.

Charlotte gestured to the TV. "It's a close game. You don't want to miss March Madness."

He straightened, inclined his head, and walked away, joining his brothers down at the other end of the bar. Good. *Fine*. That was what she'd expected.

She put him out of her mind and focused on her friends. Nearly an hour passed and she was just thinking about ordering another martini when she felt someone staring at her. She turned to find Ty's eyes locked on her instead of the game. What was his problem? She glared at him and turned away, determined to ignore him.

But no matter how funny or interesting her friends were, she kept getting distracted by the feeling she was being watched. Then she had to stop and glare at Ty until he looked away.

It was like glaring tennis.

Except she got the distinct feeling his glare was more of a *checking you out, babe,* kind of look. Super irritating.

More glaring tennis.

And more.

She thought she might be winning because he hadn't looked in a while. She deflated, not nearly as happy as she thought she'd be with the victory. A martini appeared in front of her.

"From Ty," Josh said.

She glanced over at Ty, who raised his brows before turning back to the guys. Oh, hell, she'd take a free drink. What would it hurt? She lifted the glass, took a sip, and Josh slipped a napkin in front of her with a scrawled note: *Dance with me? — Ty.*

She stared at it. *Now* he was asking her to dance? Here at a sports bar with no dance floor and no music? Was he for real?

Someone gave her hair a tug. Ty. "Well?" he asked.

She shifted to face him, trying to think of the best way to handle the situation, when he wrapped an arm around her waist and lifted her off the bar stool.

"Hey, what're you doing?" she exclaimed.

He set her on her feet and guided her away from the group, one hand on the small of her back. Halfway across the room, she dug her heels in, and they came to a dead stop.

"What do you think you're doing?" she asked, working hard to control her temper.

He held out his hand, palm up. "Dance with me. Let me make it up to you from before."

She let him have it, head swivel and all. "First, that wasn't an apology for *before*. Second, no one is dancing and I'm not into making a scene just because you feel guilty for *before*. And third, I don't appreciate being manhandled."

"Sorry for before," he said, sounding sincere.

She considered him for a moment, surprised at his sincerity, but quickly decided to cut her losses. She rejoined her friends at the bar.

Ty's voice carried across the bar. "What if I said I haven't thought about anything besides dancing with you for the last three months?"

Everyone turned to stare at him. Even Charlotte couldn't help but stare at that bold statement.

"How many beers you have, man?" Park asked from across the bar.

Ty slowly shook his head, his eyes never leaving hers.

He'd thought of nothing these past three months but dancing with her? She flushed because that was kind of romantic, even if it was his own fault they hadn't danced before.

"Slow or fast, I'm ready for ya," Ty called.

Her cheeks heated, not used to the public display of, er, interest. Her friends giggled and the guys watched Ty instead of the TV. She crossed to where Ty stood, intent on quieting him down.

He spoke first. "I should've asked you to dance three months ago at the wedding reception and I've regretted it ever since."

She could feel herself weakening at all that sincerity. Still, he'd really hurt her feelings. "You were playing a game and I told you I don't play."

"Dance with me now."

"No." She turned to go and he blocked her path.

Charlotte ground her teeth. The man had to learn a thing or two about women.

Her beauty struck him all over again up close. Long wavy brown hair with highlights, golden skin that seemed to glow, deep brown eyes, cute nose, sensuous full lips, and a killer body that could only come from a woman who valued fitness as much as he did.

"Get out of my way," Charlotte ground out.

Ty met her brown eyes sparking with anger, and offered the best words he could think of. "Please accept my sincere apology for asking everyone to dance but you at Claire and

Jake's wedding. I was playing a game, you were right, and I sincerely regret it. Your beauty caught my eye and I hoped to draw you in without coming on too strong. Sometimes I do, as you might've noticed. Anyway, it completely backfired and that's on me."

She smashed her lips together for a long moment before finally saying, "It is on you."

"Let me make it up to you. Have dinner with me. I'm in the city for a month for work." Home was LA, but he frequently flew to location in New York City for his job as a stuntman. He requested those jobs because his family was nearby in Connecticut.

"No." She shifted right to walk around him.

He stepped in her way. "Why not?"

Her eyes flashed. "You want a list of reasons?"

"You have a list?"

"We're done here." She shifted left and he stepped with her.

"See how good we would've been on the dance floor?" he asked with a grin. "It's like *Dancing with the Stars* over here."

Her lips twitched, but she forced a straight face. That little crack in her facade was all he needed. He poured on the charm, appealing to her personal-trainer side. "There's a great steakhouse in Brooklyn. You like steak, right? All that protein to build muscle."

She parked a hand on her hip. "Why do I need to build muscle?"

"I heard you were a personal trainer. Of course, you don't *need* to build muscle." He gave her an appreciative once-over in a snug dark green long-sleeve shirt and tight black jeans with high-heeled boots. She was only a few inches shorter than his own five eleven. Those long legs would feel *fantastic* wrapped around him. "Your body is amazing."

She arched a brow. "Does that normally work on your conquests?"

He shook his head. Somehow he kept screwing things up with her. "I didn't mean it bad. I used to be a personal trainer and I'm just appreciating your fitness efforts. I'll bet your core is rock solid."

She shot him an exasperated look. But the fact was, she was still standing there, so he tried another angle—super-sincere gentleman. He knew what it looked like from his dad and a few of his brothers, even if he didn't put it into regular practice.

"Charlotte," he said in a husky tone, taking her hand and tucking it in his, "I was only thinking of a nice meal and conversation. I would never see you or any other woman as a conquest." He loved women, and he'd been raised to treat them with respect. Charlotte had caught his eye at the wedding in her slinky yellow dress. Unlike most women, she actually stuck in his mind. Probably because of the fiery temper she showed when she called him on his game. She challenged him, excited him. Kind of like his stunt work, but better. No woman had interested him beyond a onetime meeting in a very long time. He couldn't wait to see her again, so when work called him back to the East Coast, he was ready to move things to a much more personal level.

She pulled her hand from his and cocked her head. "You're a smooth talker, I'll give you that, but your words lack substance."

"What do you mean?"

"I mean I don't believe that shit."

He barked out a laugh, liking her even more for her bluntness. "How about drinks?"

"No."

He took her hand and turned her in a slow twirl, like they were dancing. She went with it. "You *are* hard to get." She'd told him that at the wedding reception. He reminded her so she'd know she'd stuck in his mind.

She flashed a stunning smile and quickly shut it down. He twirled her back around and kept her hand in his. "One drink," he said. "Come on, you can do one drink."

She pulled her hand from his and studied him. He worked on a sincere gentleman expression, but it was damn hard when he was naturally up for a good time. Fast and furious was his go-to mode. He lived for the rush. It made his job perfect for him.

He gave her a slow smile. "Tempted, aren't you? Let me sweeten the deal. Drinks *and* dancing."

She pursed her lips, thinking it over. "Mad says none of her brothers can fast dance."

"Mad doesn't know everything." He leaned down to her ear. "I can't get you out of my mind. One drink, dancing after if you want, no pressure." He pulled back to look at her, hoping she'd see the sincerity in his eyes.

She blew out a long breath. "One drink."

Victory surged through him. "Great!" He pulled out his cell. "Give me your number and we'll work out a time."

"Next Thursday night, seven o'clock, after my last class at the gym," she said. No number, but at least she'd agreed to a time.

He nodded. "Yeah, I can do Thursday night. What gym?"

"It's in Clover Park. Peak Fitness. It used to be Flying Leap Fitness when Derek owned it."

"I used to work there! Cool. Is Derek still there?"

"New management. Now it's Becca. It's a women's fitness gym."

He tucked his cell into his jeans pocket. "Okay. So I'll pick you up there and we'll go—"

She held up a hand like a stop sign. "We'll have one drink of water at the gym and then I will go home."

His brows furrowed in confusion. He thought he'd been doing a victory lap here. "A drink of water," he echoed.

"Yes."

"That's our date?"

"That's your one drink." She bit back a smile, her eyes positively gleeful.

He narrowed his eyes. *Tell* me *you don't play games.* She totally played him there with her drink-of-water date.

"You don't have to come all the way out from the city for a cup of water," she added. "I completely understand."

"Oh, I'll be there."

"Sure." She strode past him, all smirky attitude.

"I will," he called after her.

"I'll hold my breath," she said with a quick glance over her shoulder.

He admired her tight ass and long legs for a mesmerizing moment before remembering himself. "Count on it."

2

Charlotte worked hard to stay focused during her last fitness class on Thursday, trying to keep thoughts of Ty from her mind. He wouldn't really drive all the way out to Connecticut from the city for a cup of water, right? That would be insane. An hour drive to Clover Park, maybe more with traffic. No man would make that much effort only to be satisfied with a drink and turn right back around. Ya know what? If he showed, it would only prove he was crazy. She didn't need crazy in her life. If he didn't show, she'd be just fine. She was much too busy to waste time obsessing over a man.

She walked up and down the rows of women in her advanced aerial hammock swing workout class. It was like yoga on a swing, low-impact with the lovely floating feeling of being in the air. The haunting, soulful music of Simrit played in the background.

"Isn't this a fun way to stretch?" she asked. The class of a dozen women, mostly in their thirties and forties, agreed with soft murmurs from where they lay on their stomachs on the swings.

She returned to her swing in the front of the room and demonstrated the next move, the bow pose. "Now grab your ankles behind you and feel your chest opening up." She watched them imitate her in the mirror. She taught a number of classes at the gym, but she liked working one-on-one with a client the best. The results were often outstanding, and she knew that was partly due to the coaching and support she offered. She'd once been in their place. Her boss, Becca, had been her personal trainer.

Twenty minutes and several poses later, she guided them to sitting lotus style on the swing. "Feel your spine lengthening and the crown of your head reaching for the sky." She closed her eyes, feeling peaceful and refreshed.

Next she guided them to the corpse pose on the mat next to their swing. They always finished with the deeply relaxing pose, lying on their backs, palms up. It was the hardest pose because it was difficult for students to fully relax.

Several moments passed in silence. She was pleased with the progress of her advanced students. Then a murmur ran through the class.

She opened her eyes. The women were whispering and staring at the doorway. *No way.* He actually showed. For a cup of water!

Ty leaned in the doorway of the room in a white sleeveless shirt and faded jeans, arms crossed. Oh man, she had a real thing for those tribal tattoos wrapped around bulging biceps. It was way too easy to imagine what those arms could do—lifting, carrying, rearranging as he pleased. She flushed at the surprisingly clear image that sprang to mind of Ty rearranging her body as he pleased. In bed.

The women were sitting up now, staring at him.

He gave them all a charming smile. "Hello, ladies. This looks like a fun workout with the swings."

"Thank you all," Charlotte said, sitting up. "I'll see you next week."

The women seemed frozen, staring at the male beauty leaning in the doorway. "Is that your boyfriend?" one woman asked.

Charlotte gave a quick head shake and remembered her hair was up in a messy ponytail. "No, he used to work here." She pulled her hair band out, slipped it on her wrist, and quickly smoothed her hair.

Ty pushed off the doorway and headed straight for her, reminding her of a wolf closing in on its prey, slow and easy before the pounce. "Charlotte promised me a drink. If the drink goes well, she might even grant me the *pleasure* of a dance."

The women tittered. Charlotte stood, fighting back a blush. That sounded so dirty.

Ty smirked. He knew it all right.

She narrowed her eyes. "I'll meet you in the hallway by the water cooler."

He smiled and laugh lines formed around his brown eyes. He was all fun and games, the near opposite of her. So why was she suddenly overheated, nerves jangling in anticipation? By the time he reached her side, she was sure everyone could see the flush in her cheeks and neck and *everywhere*.

He spoke in a warm honey tone. "It's good to see you again, Charlotte Vega."

The women *awwed* in unison. She hadn't told him her last name, so he must've been asking about her. No big deal. He only had to ask his younger sister, Mad.

She inclined her head at Ty before turning to the women. "See you next week, ladies." She hoped they'd take the hint and leave, but they stayed put, seeming entranced by Ty. She comforted herself with the knowledge that *any* woman would have this insanely lustful reaction to the man. He oozed sexual confidence and charm.

So-o-o, what to do, what to do. How to handle this awkward situation? She blinked, purposely not looking at Ty, willing her brain to work again. *Ah, yes. Work.* She shifted away from Ty, busying herself unhooking her hammock swing. She'd have them all washed for the next class.

Ty appeared at her side, towering over her in her bare feet. "Let me help you with that."

"Sure," she muttered.

They made short work of the swings, unhooking them and setting them in a large cart. He helped her fold up the mats and put them in the storage closet too. When they finished, she noticed the women from her class lingering in a group around the water cooler in the hallway, talking and sneaking looks at her and Ty.

"Time for our drink," he announced.

"Yup." For some reason she felt nervous like this was a real date or something. Absurd. They were getting a drink from the water cooler just like everyone else.

He crooked his elbow, offering his arm, the gesture taking her by surprise. She was used to men who came on strong. Not a guy who wanted to escort her in a gentlemanly way to the water cooler. She felt sort of light-headed and weird and walked straight to the door without assistance.

"I'm liking the workout clothes," he told her. She was in a T-shirt and yoga pants.

"It's my work uniform," she replied. "Well, here we are." She filled a paper cup with water and handed it to him.

He took it, somehow managing to brush his finger across the underside of her wrist at the same time. *Slick.* She knew his type. So smooth, all player all the time.

Also, her wrist sort of tingled.

She ignored that and got herself a drink.

He finished, crumpled the cup and tossed it in the small wastebasket. "Dance?"

She kept drinking her water. The women nearby had quieted, watching the exchange with interest.

"Did you enjoy the drink?" His voice was velvet, smooth and dangerously soft.

She quickly finished the water and tossed the cup in the trash. "Lovely. Thanks so much."

He took her hand. "Then it seems we should have that long-awaited dance."

She swallowed hard. There was something a little dangerous about the gleam in his eye. "I'm good, thanks."

He looked around, speaking to the group. "What do you think, ladies? I owe her a dance from a wedding where I missed my chance. Wouldn't you like to see me get that dance today?"

"Oh, yeah!" was the general consensus.

Charlotte didn't appreciate Ty involving her students like

they were putting on a show. "You want to dance so much, you go right ahead."

His smile was wicked and a little self-congratulatory like he'd won a victory. He took her hand, and she pulled away. "No, just you," she said.

"You believe this?" he asked the group with a cheerful grumble.

No one could. The women urged her to dance with him. Someone whispered, "I'll do it for you."

Ty's eyes were locked on hers. She crossed her arms.

He let out a big sigh. "I do owe you a dance. Okay, fine. Put on whatever's on your playlist."

"Sure thing," she said. "We'd all love to watch you dance." There was no way any man would dance in front of a group of women by himself. Besides, he could probably only slow dance. "Probably be a fast dance," she added.

One corner of his mouth lifted. "Awesome."

She stared at him. *You serious?*

He jerked his chin. *Watch me.*

The silent communication freaked her out, like they were actually in tune with each other or something. She whirled and went back in the workout room to her cell phone and clicked over to her personal workout playlist. It would synch to the speaker dock. The women trailed behind them, watching with open curiosity.

Ty came up behind her, his heat warming her back. She had the strangest urge to lean back and just melt into him. He reached around her to hold the cell and check out her music. His forearm had a long thin scar and ropey muscle. She stared at that scar, wondering how many he had from doing stunts. A flutter of worry for his safety joined the butterflies in her stomach. Her brain was fuzzy, addled with his proximity and his woodsy, musky outdoor sex scent.

He read over her shoulder, his breath running hot over her ear. "'SexyBack' by Justin Timberlake? I'd love to."

"Maybe something less, um..." She quickly scrolled through the rest of her playlist for a less sexy song. *No, not that one, ooh, definitely not that one.* Apparently she favored sexy songs.

His voice dropped to a husky register. "You dirty girl."

She whirled.

Ty gave her a smirky knowing look. "Put on 'SexyBack,' unless you're afraid of what you might see."

"I'm not afraid," she muttered, pulling the song up and hitting play.

Ty strutted toward the center of the room and turned, his dark eyes heated and locked on hers. She held her breath, wondering if he'd make a fool of himself, and what did that say about him if he was willing to do that for her?

He did a sensuous full body wave and then he snagged the bottom of his shirt with one hand, lifting as he moved in another full body wave. Holy hotness. She stared at each inch of exposed tanned skin as ridged abs, pecs, and enormous shoulders came fully into view. He pulled the shirt off and tossed it to her.

A cheer went up. Not from her. She was speechless. The shirt bounced off her limp hand and hit the floor.

The women rushed to where she stood to get a better view of Ty. "Oh, yeah, baby!" they cheered. "Take it all off!"

"Ladies!" she exclaimed.

Ty grinned and kept dancing, doing some chest pops, turning to the side for a sensuous body wave, and then facing front, arms crisscrossing as his hips circled. She broke out in a sweat. Omigod, he was actually good. Beyond good. It was like her own personal *Magic Mike*. The movie about male strippers was also a dance revue in Vegas now.

He slid to the right, did a jump crisscrossing of his legs for a quick spin, and then hit the floor, landing in a plank position. He did some slow push-ups, legs spread wide that showed every muscular line of his back, and then added some hip action that looked like he was fucking—

His eyes locked on hers. Hot. Penetrating. *Fuck me.*

"I'd fuck him if I was single," the woman next to her replied.

Oh, shit, had Charlotte said that fuck-me part out loud?

Ty flipped to his back, sitting, hands on the floor, legs apart, and then slowly thrusting upward, once, twice, three times before springing to his feet. *My own personal sex dance.* The women were going nuts, cheering him on and catcalling. She suddenly wished it was just the two of them. His heated gaze always returned to her, holding her under his spell. He kept his jeans on, but the hip action on this guy left no question how he'd be in the bedroom. Ty's dancing showed off all of his best features—shoulders, chest, abs, basically everything. He was fucking spectacular. If dance was foreplay, she was ready to go. The song ended suddenly and he finished—

With a backflip!

The entire room gasped in shock and then broke into applause. Charlotte shut her open jaw with a snap. Omigod. She couldn't believe he had those kind of moves.

Ty grinned, took a bow, and jogged over to her. "How'd I do?"

"Wonderful!" the women enthused.

"Charlotte?" Ty prompted.

She gazed at the drop of sweat trickling down his chest to a dark arrow leading to the bulge in his jeans. She licked her lips, wanting to trace every muscular line of his body with her tongue.

Ty took her hand and kissed the back of it. "We had our drink, we had our dance, how about a sunset dinner cruise on my yacht?"

"Yes!" the women chorused.

"Oh, Charlotte, you have to go," one woman said. "Do it for us!"

She met his warm gaze, still a little stunned at his performance. "How did you learn to dance like that?"

He leaned close, his voice rumbling in her ear, giving her a hot shiver. "My friend dragged me to a workshop with the choreographer for the *Magic Mike* movies. He wanted to audition for the Las Vegas show. The backflip was all me. Did you like?"

He pulled back to look at her and she nodded automatically. His bare muscular chest and massive shoulders were doing what no man had done for her in a very long time. A raw aching need combined with pure liquid heat.

She had to touch. Her hand settled on his warm chest.

His large hand covered hers, holding it there. "Would you do me the honor of going on a sunset cruise? I'll make you dinner. It's a beautiful yacht—"

"Yes," she said softly, completely taken in by his charm, his extraordinary effort for a date, and all that sweet sincerity.

The women cheered. She dropped her hand from Ty's beautiful chest, coming back to herself to address their audience. "Okay, ladies. Show's over."

Ty snagged his shirt from the floor and pulled it back on. "Saturday. I'll pick you up at four thirty." He gave her a quick kiss on the cheek and swaggered toward the door.

Charlotte stood there for a full minute watching him go. Then she moved in a daze, closing up the room for the night, still not quite believing what had just happened.

By the time she got home, she'd sobered considerably. She reminded herself not to get too caught up in his charm. This would just be one fun date. He lived in LA; she lived here. There was no real possibility of a relationship.

Besides, if he knew what was really going on with her, he'd be running for the hills.

3

———

Ty pulled up to Charlotte's ranch home in a 1966 cherry-red Mustang convertible he'd borrowed from his best friend and honorary brother Park. Ty had to go all out with Charlotte to reverse the terrible first impression he'd made. He snagged the bouquet of yellow flowers that reminded him of the awesome dress she'd worn the first time he'd clapped eyes on her. He'd first noticed her long legs in the dress, but the rest of her was amazing too—glossy long hair, glowing skin, big breasts, narrow waist, curvy hips, shapely ass. And that was just her looks. Her fierceness and strength excited him, but he'd also noticed a softness, maybe a bit of longing when she'd finally granted him the honor of a date. She was smart, loyal to her friends, and probably more great stuff. That was as much as he could get out of Mad about Charlotte before Mad hollered at him to just spend time with Charlotte and shut up with the questions.

He headed to the front door, an unusual surge of adrenaline amping him up. He didn't usually get worked up over first dates. He blew out a breath and rang the bell. The door opened a moment later to Charlotte with her long hair up in a high ponytail, looking cute and young. She wore a billowy peach shirt with an elastic waist over white pants that ended mid-calf. And the best part—high-heeled tan sandals with skinny ties that wrapped around her ankles. Sexy as sin. His gaze lingered on peach toenails, and then, remembering his manners, he met her deep brown eyes. "You look beautiful. These are for you." He handed her the flowers.

"Thanks," she said softly, staring at the flowers for a long moment. She stepped back. "Come in for a minute while I put these in a vase."

He stepped inside to a living room with a black leather sofa, round glass coffee table, and bright red area rug. The walls were sky blue; the windows had sheer white drapes. He liked it, not too girly, bold like the woman. He rocked on his heels. They were going to have a blast on the yacht. He'd borrowed it from an actor friend, Will, who Ty had met on a movie set years ago. The forty-two-foot yacht was worth a cool half mil with a wet bar, galley kitchen, air-conditioned salon with TV and cushy sofas, two bathrooms, and two bedrooms. The master bedroom featured a wall of mirrors and he'd love to put them to use. Naked.

He blew out a breath, trying to think of anything but his lust for Charlotte. The last thing he wanted was to start the date with a woody. He mentally reviewed the lesson he'd had last weekend in captaining the boat. Will had supervised while Ty steered them down the Hudson River during the party. The calm open waters were no challenge at all. Ty had driven speedboats tons of times for movie stunts. He'd sworn on his life to have it back in one piece. No problemo. He only planned a short trip up and down the Harlem River, close to where it was now docked in Manhattan. Then he'd set anchor, make dinner, and hopefully a little slow dancing and some loving below deck. It was the natural course of events for all of his dates. After the smoldering looks Charlotte shot him after his Magic Mike-style dance, he was pretty sure she'd be into it too.

Charlotte appeared in the living room. "All set."

"Great." He followed her out the door. She locked up, turned, and gasped.

"Is this yours?" she asked, heading over to the car.

"I borrowed it from Park," he said, opening the passenger door for her. "You like classic cars?"

"I love Mustangs!" She slid inside and he shut the door.

When he got in the driver's side, he turned to her. "You want the top down?" It was the first weekend of April and on the warm side for this time of year in Connecticut, a comfortable seventy degrees.

"Absolutely," she said.

He turned on the car and brought the top down. Charlotte stretched her arms straight up out of the top of the car, lifting her face to the sun with a blissful smile. She dropped her arms and turned to him, still smiling. He couldn't breathe for a moment. She was a looker, but when she smiled at him like that, stunningly beautiful. He had the sudden urge to kiss her, but she shifted, facing front.

"Let's roll," she said cheerfully.

"You got it." He backed out of the driveway and headed to the city. He asked her about her day and then dove right into the getting-to-know-you questions. He always asked a lot of questions because women loved sharing. "So tell me about you. Did you grow up around here?"

"I grew up in Jersey."

"A Jersey girl, huh? Heard they're the wild ones."

"Where'd you hear that?"

"From another Jersey girl. I had no choice but to believe her when she danced topless on the bar."

"Uh-huh."

He sensed a considerable cooling in her. "Kidding." Actually that had happened, but he shouldn't have brought up another woman. "Back to you. How'd you get into personal training?"

"I worked with a great trainer. She inspired me. What made you get into it?"

"I was a gym rat and they offered to hire me. That was back when they let men into the place. I liked it, but I was too restless to stay in the routine. One of the guys I trained was a retired stuntman and hooked me up in LA. I haven't looked back since. I love it."

"Is it really dangerous?" She actually sounded worried.

He stopped at a traffic light and met her eyes. "There's some danger, yes. But the outfit I work with is a small group of well-trained stuntmen and women. Plus, I'm like a cat. Nine lives."

"How many have you spent?"

"Probably eight." He laughed. He'd had a few close calls, a couple of broken bones, but he always came out on top.

"What kind of stunts do you do?"

"All different stuff. That's what I like about it. Never a dull day. I do motorcycle stuff like jumps, spinouts, riding down stairs."

"That must be bumpy."

"Yeah, it's rough. And then, you know, the usual car chases, jumping out windows, rappelling down buildings, an occasional fight sequence if they don't want to chance the actor getting hurt. I'm a blackbelt. Actually I love fight scenes best. Pure fun."

"You sound like your sister. Mad loves sparring."

He glanced up to see the light was green and hit the accelerator. "I'm the one that got her into my dojo. I've sparred with her before. She's good for her size."

"Yeah, she taught us some self-defense moves."

"Good, everyone should know that stuff."

She was quiet, and he glanced over to find her staring at him, a small smile playing over her lips.

"What?" he asked.

"I still can't believe that dance you did! That was incredible."

He grinned. "You want a repeat performance?"

"Hell yeah! I wouldn't mind seeing that again."

"No problem. Back to you, what do you do in your free time? Any hobbies?" He was working up to what he really wanted to know—her boyfriend history. Some women were bitter, closed off, and he didn't even attempt a relationship. He wasn't exactly sure where she landed on that spectrum. She seemed at times quick to slam on the brakes, keeping him at a safe distance, and then, other times, like now, warm and open.

He glanced over at her, speaking animatedly about nutrition and fitness, gesturing with her hands as she spoke. She sure had a lot of energy.

But once they moved off that topic, she was surprisingly close-lipped, frequently turning the question back to him or changing the subject. He had the uneasy feeling she was hiding something. Or maybe she was just a very private person.

Either way, he was itching to know more about the mysterious Charlotte Vega.

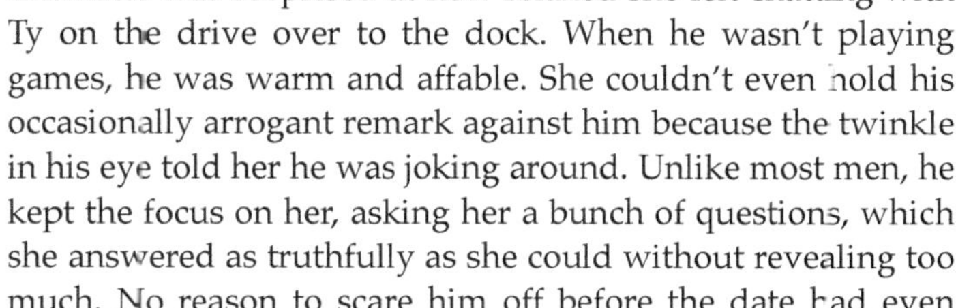

Charlotte was surprised at how relaxed she felt chatting with Ty on the drive over to the dock. When he wasn't playing games, he was warm and affable. She couldn't even hold his occasionally arrogant remark against him because the twinkle in his eye told her he was joking around. Unlike most men, he kept the focus on her, asking her a bunch of questions, which she answered as truthfully as she could without revealing too much. No reason to scare him off before the date had even begun. Anyway, she wasn't a big sharer with men or women, used to keeping her problems to herself. Ty seemed fine with her cagey responses, never pushing for more.

"You're awfully quiet all of a sudden," Ty said. "Too many questions?"

"No, it's nice that you care."

"Anything you want to ask about me?"

"I was wondering one thing." It had been bugging her for a while now. Earlier this year, when Ty's younger sister, Mad, and Park finally got together, Ty had butted in and told Park to back off. Mad was a close friend of Charlotte's from book club and Charlotte had been outraged on her friend's behalf.

"Shoot," he said.

"Why'd you get between Mad and Park? Anyone could see how in love with him she is."

"It was my duty as a big brother."

"It's your duty to deny your sister her true love?"

"I was protecting her," he said simply. "Park wasn't serious and she was."

"It really hurt her when he backed off."

He pulled off the exit into the city. "Yeah, but it would've hurt her more if he messed around with her and bailed. I nipped it in the bud and then Park had to step up if Mad was really what he wanted. He stepped up, asked her to marry him, she's happy, so I'm happy."

"And if he didn't?"

"Then I saved her a lot of heartbreak."

"Or you might've destroyed any chance of happiness." Love was a fragile, delicate thing, Charlotte always thought. You had to be so careful or *bam!* The whole thing would blow up in your face.

He glanced over at her. "Look, I love Park like a brother, we go way back, but that doesn't mean I'd let him or anyone hurt Mad. You don't know the bad place she was in when he left for the Air Force. She was so upset she got herself in all kinds of trouble at school and at home. The Mad you know today is in a much better place. I wasn't going to stand by and watch her spiral out of control again."

She was quiet, considering that. She hadn't known Mad back then, only the last two years from book club. Mad was tough, smart, and fearless, but Charlotte could see how the woman might get herself in deep. Mad was one of those secretly sensitive souls.

Ty went on. "Something you have to understand about Mad, and me too, I guess. Upset feelings quickly translate to anger. That's why I got her into my dojo. If you control that energy, it can be a force for good. She helped a lot of people up their game with her aggressive sparring."

"Aren't you philosophical?"

He chuckled.

"It all sounds more reasonable when you explain it like that. From the outside it just looked like you were being a buttinski."

"Charlotte, you wound me." He grinned, the smile lighting up his face. "I *always* have good intentions. Whether or not that comes out the right way is another story."

"Good to know."

When they arrived at the dock, Charlotte stared in awe at a gorgeous white yacht with an open area on the top level for driving it, an enclosed cabin on the main level with adjoining decks on the front and back, and then on the lower level a series of portholes, probably for sleeping quarters. What a fantastic party boat!

"This is yours?" she exclaimed. "Stunt work must pay more than I thought."

His chest puffed out as he admired the boat. "It pays well, but I borrowed it from my friend Will. Come on, let's go."

Borrowed? She followed hot on his heels. "Wait, do you know how to drive it?"

He laughed and unlocked the gate to the plank thingy. "You don't *drive* a boat. You captain it. And, yes, I can captain it. Don't worry, I operate tons of vehicles at work, including speedboats."

He boarded the boat and she followed behind, staring at the small insulated cooler he carried. Her stomach growled. She'd worked today and hadn't had a chance to grocery shop, so she'd saved her appetite for their sunset dinner cruise.

"What're we having for dinner?" she asked.

"It's a surprise." He gestured toward the front of the boat, where two fully reclined loungers waited. "Go relax on the deck while I put the food away." He headed inside the cabin, where she guessed the kitchen was. She peeked in the windows on her way to the deck, checking out a living room with a long sofa on one side and a love seat on the other adjoining a galley kitchen. Cool!

She adjusted one of the loungers to an upright position and took a seat, already enjoying the view of the river with the bridges and buildings in the distance. This would be awesome. She shivered. It was already cooling down. She should've brought a light jacket. Ty wasn't wearing one either. Like her, he was dressed for spring in a T-shirt and jeans. Hopefully they'd spend most of their time hanging out in the enclosed living room.

She glanced around. Ty was untying the boat from the dock. She waited to see where he went and saw him emerge a few minutes later on the top level, the central control area of the boat. She quickly followed, eager to see how all the controls worked.

"Hey, Captain," she said.

He turned with a smile, and she gave him a jaunty salute. "Hey, gorgeous. At ease."

She laughed and joined him by the dashboard or control panel, whatever it was called. She wasn't too nautical. She'd only been on a boat once, the ferry that went from New Jersey to the Statue of Liberty crowded with tourists. This was much cooler.

Ty hit a few buttons, consulted a map, and then slowly pulled away from the dock. She checked her cell. Six o'clock. Sunset would probably be around seven thirty; then she figured they'd turn back around. He'd promised a sunset cruise. It wouldn't be too fun to be out on the river at night. Cold and dark.

She crossed her arms, rubbing them for warmth. "Getting chilly already."

Ty laughed, looking comfortable at the wheel. "It's not chilly. It's refreshing." He gave her ponytail a tug. "Woman up."

"You have more body mass to keep you warm," she returned.

He snagged her around the waist and pulled her in front of him while he steered, his arms around her on the wheel. This was definitely warmer, maybe a little too warm. Heat at her back, strong warm arms around her, woodsy outdoor sex scent surrounding her.

She tried for an unaffected tone. "So where are we headed on this sunset cruise, Captain?"

He dipped his head near her ear, his voice a low rumble that gave her a delicious shiver. "Figured we'd head down the river a bit and then stop somewhere to cook dinner."

"You want any help?"

He straightened. "Nope. I got it all under control."

She believed him and actually relaxed, happy to let someone else do all the work. "Awesome."

She enjoyed the view as they motored along, passing a few smaller boats on their way down the river. Her stomach growled loudly.

"You hungry?" he asked.

She put a hand to her stomach with a laugh. "Yes. I normally have a protein snack in the afternoon, but I ran out and didn't have time to grocery shop. I have hypoglycemia, so I get low blood sugar. As long as I eat in the next hour or so, I'll be fine."

"What happens if you don't?"

"Sometimes I get a little shaky, but usually I just get really irritable."

"Ooh, boy, don't want a hangry woman on board." He stepped away to consult a map, his brows scrunching together in concentration.

She grabbed the wheel. "Should I steer while you look at the map?"

"Sure," he said absently.

Oh, this was cool. Driving down the middle of the river. Or cruising. Whatever it was called.

Ty studied the map for a really long time before turning back to her. "I think there's a cove just up ahead where we can anchor while I cook."

"Cool."

He took his place back at the wheel, keeping her warm in the circle of his arms. They cruised for a good half hour before they reached the cove. Not exactly "just up ahead," as Ty had said. He shifted her to the side, telling her he needed to focus on steering.

Ty directed the yacht into the cove and then turned the wheel, shifting their position so they'd face out of the cove. They didn't quite make it in a complete turn before the boat made a weird grinding noise.

"Shit," he said.

"What's wrong?"

He kept trying to maneuver the boat, gunning the engine, and the sound got worse and really loud, and then they came to a dead stop. "Fuck."

"What?"

"We're stuck. It's not responding." He crossed to the side of the boat and looked down. "I'd better get below."

She followed him down the stairs and they both peered over the railing. The "cove" looked more like a swamp and they appeared to be mired in mud. And the stench, omigod. Some combination of garbage, sewer, and rotting plant life. She switched to breathing through her mouth.

Ty covered his nose and mouth with his arm, breathing through the fabric of his shirt sleeve.

"Just hit the gas hard and get us out of here," she said.

He nodded once and headed back up to the boat's control center. She followed, not wanting to stay close to the stench. Ty worked every angle, but it was a no go. Just lots of horrible grinding noises.

He looked at her with a horrified expression. "I can't screw up the engine. This yacht is worth more than I can repay. Like a half mil."

"Just use your captaining skill to get us out of here!" she exclaimed. Panic set in. She could *not* be stuck on this boat for hours with the man who oozed sex and charm and heart-squeezing sincerity. Maybe they'd be stuck all night!

They'd have to use each other for body heat, she thought darkly. She'd get sucked in. She wasn't supposed to get sucked in. This was definitely not the right time in her life for *any* kind of sucking. She pressed her fingers to her temples. That sounded dirty. It was the Ty effect. She had serious decisions to make for her future and Ty could never be part of any of that.

She paced, already feeling trapped. This was supposed to be one fun date! Just dinner, maybe a goodnight kiss. She wanted light fun with Ty on her terms. These were not her terms!

She stopped pacing and stared at Ty, who was staring at the controls. "Do something!"

He mumbled something that sounded like *map.*

"What're you saying?"

He spoke up. "I must've read the map wrong. Will uses these weird nautical maps."

"Doesn't everyone that drives a boat?" she screeched. She felt like smacking Ty for getting them into this situation. He had no business taking them out on this boat when he didn't know what he was doing.

He made a palms-down gesture of *let's take it down a notch.* "It's okay. I'll just…okay, everything will be okay. Stay calm. Let's think this through."

"I'm not spending the night on this boat with you."

"This is no problem. You go relax on a deck chair while I figure this out."

She scowled and crossed her arms. "I cannot believe you invited me on a borrowed boat that you have no idea how to drive."

He spoke through his teeth. "I'm *captaining* it. Not driving. And this isn't operator error."

"It *is* operator error. Otherwise, we wouldn't be stuck in a swamp."

He shoved a hand in his hair. "I'm just not used to nautical maps."

Grr…same difference. They were stuck.

She watched as Ty tried to shift them forward, reverse, sideways, everything seemed to make it worse. The boat dug deeper in the mud and the engine sounded like it was about to give up the fight and die on them.

"Stop!" she finally hollered. "You're just getting us in deeper. Call the Coast Guard."

He stopped. "Good idea. So let's see." He pulled his cell phone from his jeans pocket. "Would that be nine-one-one, or ya think they have a special number?"

She looked around and spotted the radio clipped overhead. She pulled it down. "I think you're supposed to talk into this."

"Oh, hey, there's a distress button. That's convenient. I'll just press that." He pressed the button and waited. Nothing happened. He pressed it for a long time, released it, and the thing beeped. He turned to her. "They probably know where we are already from the GPS."

"Why didn't you use the GPS to navigate?"

"It seemed like a simple trip," he replied.

She bit back a snarky remark. Of course, confident Ty would assume he could handle everything. She had to remain calm. Snark wouldn't help them out of this situation. They had to work together.

"You think the radio is connected to the GPS?" Ty asked.

"I don't know. I know nothing about boats."

He stared at the radio as if it might have the answer. He pressed the button a third time, saying, "Mayday, Mayday, we're stuck in mud—" he paused and looked over at her like maybe she knew what to say because *he* sure as hell didn't "—uh, over."

Static crackled and then a man answered, asking for their location. Ty looked around. "It's the cove off the Harlem river."

The guy asked for the latitude and longitude coordinates. Ty studied the map for a long time before saying, "It looks like east? It's definitely to the right on the map. Maybe an inch from some green area. I think it's a park."

Charlotte's hopes for a rescue plummeted.

4

———

Charlotte stepped out on the deck and walked the perimeter of the boat. Oh, man, they were in deep, surrounded on all sides by mud. They were pretty much screwed. How had he even gotten them this far into the swamp? They weren't all that close to shore either.

"Looks like you're stuck!" someone hollered.

She looked over to a park on shore, where they'd attracted a crowd of curious onlookers. Lots of people having barbeques and picnics. "Yeah, we're stuck!" she hollered back. "We called the Coast Guard!"

"That sucks," a man said. More people gathered, pointing and talking about them.

She turned away, telling herself this would be okay. Even though Ty couldn't figure out where they were nautically, they were close enough to shore for people to help. Maybe they'd get a rowboat out to them or a helicopter or something. No, probably a helicopter wouldn't work. Well, *some-thing* had to work because she was absolutely *not* spending the night with Ty on this boat.

She suddenly realized the boat was quiet. The engine was off. She headed back up to the control area to find out why. "You cut the engine, or did it die?"

Ty grimaced. "The guy on the radio said I should turn it off, so…uh, I did. And…"

"What?" she asked, already dreading whatever he was going to say next.

"Turns out the Coast Guard won't help us."

"They won't help us," she echoed.

He slowly shook his head. "We're not an emergency. Not sinking, no fire, no injuries. They said just wait for high tide. Local cops are going to get a boat guy out to us then to help." He glanced over to the crowd of curious people at the nearby park. "This is a little embarrassing, isn't it?"

"It'll be a lot *less* embarrassing if we can get out of here. When's high tide?"

"They estimate approximately twelve fifteen."

"Tonight? You mean midnight? We're stuck here for six hours?"

He rubbed the back of his neck. "Yeah, and then the rescue will take a while. They need to row out to us and some expert guy who knows boats is going to maneuver us out, so-o-o, yeah. Sorry."

"Sorry," she echoed numbly.

He gave her ponytail a tug. "Hey, it won't be that bad. We can find something to do, right? Just you and me stranded?" He raised his brows suggestively.

Charlotte ignored that, desperate for a better solution. "Why don't you use your stuntman skills to jump off this boat, wade through the mud, and rescue us?"

"Sugar, I know I'm built for strength, but even I can't push a yacht out of mud."

"Then you can…" She gestured wildly. "You can wade to shore, get a rowboat, and rescue me."

"Are you serious?"

"Do I look like I'm playing?" she shouted.

He huffed. "Fine."

He headed down to the lower deck and she followed, hoping he'd pull through with his stunt skills. She peered down at the mud—dead rotting fish and a couple cans of beer.

Ty leaned over the deck railing and then did a tour around the perimeter, inspecting the mud from all sides just like she'd done earlier. He appeared back at her side. "It must be deep. You really want me jumping into this?"

"I really do," she assured him.

He held her chin with a warm tender gaze. "I'd love to play hero for you."

Her breath caught, surprised at the unexpected sweetness.

He dropped his hand and turned back to the mud. "Let me test it first. Never jump into a risky situation without knowing all the outcomes."

"Uh-huh."

He looked around and found a long pole with a curved hook attached to the side of the boat. He hauled it over the deck railing, pole first, and plunged it into the mud. She watched as it sank deep and then the mud seemed to be sucking it deeper.

"Fuck, it's like quicksand," he said, straining mightily to retrieve the pole. "If I get pulled under, there's no way to rescue me or you."

Dammit.

He wrestled with the pole and finally yanked it free. Mud splattered all over Ty, the deck, and the side of the boat. She jumped back just in time.

He looked down at himself and then to her. He grimaced. "I need a change of clothes."

She waved a hand in front of her nose. "You need a shower."

He strode over to the far end of the boat and she followed automatically. "I don't want to get their fancy bathroom dirty," he said before pulling off the shirt, his muscles rippling with the movement. *Man candy wrapped in bacon.* Damn, she must really be hungry if she was fantasizing about a bacon-wrapped Ty. She was losing brain cells just looking at him. The muscle definition was spectacular—large rounded shoulders, bulging biceps covered in tribal tattoos, pecs and ridged abs tapering to a narrow waist. He kicked off his sneakers.

"Wait!" she blurted in a belated attempt at self-preservation. "What if the shower doesn't work with the engine off?"

"It'll work for a short while." He stripped out of his socks and then his jeans. She got a brief glimpse of deep red boxer briefs with an impressive bulge and legs thick with muscle before she turned away. Ty kept talking. "Will's wife wouldn't stay overnight with the kids until she was sure it was rigged for a shower no matter what. I'm heading downstairs. Can you look around for a robe for me in the master bedroom?"

She spoke without turning around. "Sure. I'll just give you a few minutes to get settled."

"Stairs are right off the kitchen."

She heard the door to the enclosed cabin open and close and waited on deck. She peeked at his pile of muddy clothes and saw the red boxer briefs on top. Oh-kay, guess the mud soaked through enough to bother him, so-o-o, that happened. She waited until she was sure he was safely in the shower and headed inside the cabin. Thankfully, it was a little warmer in the cabin than outside. She crossed through the living room to the galley kitchen and down the adjacent spiral staircase. Now why did Ty ask for a robe? He should wear clothes, the more of him covered, the better. Her willpower reserves would only weaken as the night wore on. Why make it harder on herself?

She found a bedroom with a couple of little girl outfits in it and quickly moved over to the master bedroom. Yes! She found some men's shorts, boxers, a polo shirt, and a cardigan. She stopped to check the size because they looked kind of small. Men's medium. That must be why Ty asked for a robe. He knew he wouldn't fit in his friend's stuff. She set everything on top of the dresser and pulled on the olive green cardigan, buttoning it. Ooh, soft as cashmere. Hello, she was on a yacht. It probably was cashmere. She kept looking through drawers and a closet, delusionally hopeful to cover Ty. She found a black silk robe and draped it over her shoulder. It would have to do. She held up the boxers, wondering if they would fit since they were baggy with a stretchy elastic waistband.

"No way I'm wearing another guy's boxers," Ty boomed. She jumped and whirled to face him where he now stood in the bedroom, wearing only a white towel around his waist. Geez, the man was like sculpted marble. Beyond any man she'd ever seen in real life. Only two scars marred his tanned skin, one on his forearm, one on his rib. Even that was sexy; he was a glorious sculpted badass. He headed straight for her, a walking aphrodisiac. She stood perfectly still, all rational thought deserting her as he closed the distance between them. He smelled so good now, fresh and clean, his dark hair slicked back. Of course, that only emphasized his chiseled cheekbones and stubbled jaw. His lips formed a smirk. Caught in the act of ogling!

She looked away, burning with lust, no sense denying it. Ty was the definition of male beauty—solid, powerful, large *everywhere. Mmm, yes.*

No!

This had disaster written all over it.

He plucked the robe from her shoulder. "Thanks."

"Yes, I found a robe," she said unnecessarily to the ceiling. *Come on, brain, get back on board!* She shoved the boxers back in a drawer.

"I noticed." She could hear the smile in his voice, but didn't trust herself with another peek at perfection.

"Meet you upstairs," she muttered and took off.

She made a small tour of the enclosed living room/kitchen space, taking deep calming breaths. Ooh, a flat-screen TV right across from the cushy beige sofa. Then she remembered they had no power. She glanced at the now useless kitchen with its refrigerator, microwave, and stove. They also had no way to cook dinner. She checked her cell. After seven.

Ty appeared in the silk robe, his shoulders straining the fabric, but he did manage to tie it with the belt. It ended high up on his thigh. The white towel peeked out underneath. Kind of like a terrycloth kilt. She swallowed. She had a real thing for men in kilts. Not that she'd ever seen one in real life, only in romance novels. This was more like a sultan in silk with hints of Greek toga and Scottish kilt—

Ty interrupted her squirrely line of thinking. "The robe should work as long as I don't stretch or move too much. Let's see what we can do about dinner."

She brightened, glad to focus on food, and joined him in the kitchen. He opened the refrigerator—empty except for the lone insulated cooler of food Ty had brought. He snagged the cooler, unzipping it so she could see—a plastic container of spaghetti sauce and a box of raw spaghetti.

"Guess I can't cook the spaghetti," he said, "but we could eat cold sauce."

She took the sauce container out and tapped the frosty lid. "Frozen." He'd left the ice pack in the cooler's mesh pocket.

"Sauce popsicles?" he asked with a grin.

"Sure, I'd love to take turns licking a sauce cube," she said drily.

"I'd love to watch you lick my cube."

She stared at him, not amused.

"It's not actually cubic." He snorted. "That sounds…" He stopped himself and cleared his throat. "Anyway, the sauce is good. Will's wife made it." He took the container from her and tapped it in a few places, checking to make sure it was really frozen, she supposed. He set the container on the counter. "It'll thaw pretty quick, right?"

"I don't know."

The beginnings of a low-blood-sugar headache made the reality of no food and no power stuck in the cold swamp hit her all at once. A dark cloud of irritation settled over her. This was quite possibly the worst first date she'd ever been on and she'd been on plenty of nightmare dates. One date even brought his mother to interview her (he later informed her she didn't get the mom stamp of approval).

Think positive. First things first. Find something to eat. Surely once she ate, she'd have the resources to deal with whatever was ahead.

"Search the cabinets," she said.

"Sure," he said in an entirely too cheerful tone. "Let's see what we can scrounge up."

She got to work. Empty, empty, dishes, assorted ketchup and mustard packets, and, in a high cabinet, a small Ziploc bag with an opened bag of jellybeans inside. She pulled it out and eyed the jellybeans. Her doctor told her not to eat sugar because it made her hypoglycemia worse. She'd felt tons better since kicking the sugar habit, more energy, less moody, no more headaches.

Ty appeared at her side. "Oh, yeah. Those jellybeans were supposed to be for Will's kid for Easter, but then he couldn't resist and had a few. Of course, he couldn't bring an opened bag home—clear admission of guilt—so he stashed it in the high cabinet." At her silence, he added, "Don't worry. He got a fresh bag for his daughter."

"Did you find anything?" she asked, putting the jellybeans back.

"No. We pretty much cleaned it out last weekend at the party."

She berated herself for not replenishing her purse with a snack. She'd been in a hurry today after working and then getting ready for the mud date. *Augh!* She could feel her blood sugar plummeting, making her feel weak and fatigued. Her headache was getting worse too. She hated feeling like this.

She headed back to the sofa, where she'd left her large purse, hoping something was hiding in its depths. She really didn't want to get shaky, that was the worst. She dug around, hunting for a half-eaten granola bar or a few almonds. Nothing.

Damn, damn, damn.

Damn him for putting her in this situation and damn her for not being better prepared. This never would've happened if she hadn't fallen for the sexy moves of a stripper dance. She should know better. Look what had happened to her mom, after all.

5

Ty searched high and low in every spot he could think of for something to feed Charlotte. She was slumped on the sofa, arms crossed tight across her growling stomach, her lips pressed in a flat line. Terribly hangry but still sexy as hell even in Will's sweater. This was maybe the all-time worst date he'd ever taken someone on. It had started out so promising and he'd been pretty sure he was reversing the awful first impression he'd made. At least the swamp smell didn't reach inside the cabin. Maybe just a faint whiff. He snagged the jellybeans, determined to get some into her. This would be a really long wait stuck on a boat with a hangry woman.

He flopped next to her on the sofa. "How about strip jellybeans? We take off one item of clothing of the other person's choosing for each piece of candy."

She made a weird growl deep in her throat and he quickly switched gears. "Or you could just have one." He snagged a red jellybean, holding it out to her.

She didn't take it. "My doctor told me to avoid sugar. It messes too much with my blood sugar levels."

"Are you diabetic?"

"No. The reverse. Hypoglycemia."

"Oh, yeah. You mentioned that earlier. Will it kill you?"

"No."

"Permanently damage you?"

"No, but I know it'll mess with my sugar levels and then I'll get shaky with the sugar crash."

"We'll keep a nice even supply, regular sugar infusions. These are extenuating circumstances." When she didn't reply, he tried another tactic. "How about this? A kiss for each jellybean I feed you."

"Where do you get these ridiculous ideas?" she exclaimed, her hands waving wildly. "Do you think being hungry and stuck on a boat in the middle of a swamp for six plus hours with no power is making me hot?"

He cocked his head like he was considering it. "I'm guessing no?" He didn't mind her letting off a little steam. He'd probably do the same if the situation was reversed. He held up the jellybean. "What can I do to entice you to eat this jellybean?"

"Serve it to me with steak?"

He popped the jellybean in his mouth and chewed. "See, now I offered to take you to a steakhouse, but you turned that date down." That had been his first idea back when he'd seen her at Garner's, but he'd had to go bigger to get her attention. "If you think about it, none of this is really my fault."

Her death glare was impressively fierce. Not enough to scare him off, but…honestly, kind of a turn-on.

"I'm thinking about kissing you soon," he informed her. He'd thought of little else since he'd picked her up at her house. Now, stuck in mud, hangry or not, he couldn't deny he still wanted to very much. Her lips were deliciously sensual. Luscious even. He'd bet she tasted sweet too.

"Think again," she growled.

Clearly she wasn't on the same dirty line of thinking as he was. He'd have to work on that. He suddenly realized the room was getting darker. "Looks like the sun's setting."

"No shit."

He grinned. "So what happens on the dark boat stays on the dark boat. Nudge, wink."

She pursed her lips. "You're not as funny as you think you are."

He snagged another jellybean, popped it in his mouth, and chewed. "Mmm, coconut."

She stood. "We need to look for a flashlight."

He dropped the jellybean bag on the coffee table and joined her in the search. He found a headlamp in a kitchen drawer. He turned it on and put the headband on.

"How's this?" he asked, turning to where she was looking through kitchen cabinets.

She shielded her eyes. "Nice and nerdy."

He quickly took it off and tossed it back in the drawer.

She rummaged through the cabinet under the sink and pulled out a black flashlight. "This'll have to do." She turned it on, playing with the light levels, high and low.

"You'd better keep it on low so the batteries don't run out."

She clicked it to low and set it on the coffee table, facing up. They still had some light from the sun, not much, and the flashlight lit the room almost like a candle would.

He watched as she paced from kitchen to living room over and over. Kinda reminded him of a caged animal. Like him, she was a physical person and used to a lot of activity, which made the small enclosed space difficult to tolerate. Knowing they were stuck made it even worse. He got it. He really did, which was exactly why he'd taken a long run earlier today. He was about to suggest she do some push-ups when she surprised him, suddenly throwing herself facedown on the sofa. Oh shit. Was she crying?

He rushed over and knelt next to the sofa. "Don't cry."

"I'm not crying," she said in a small heartbreakingly sad voice. "I don't cry when I get frustrated. Normally I fight, but I'm weak from lack of food."

He rubbed her back for a moment in sympathy, and she stayed just like she was, flopped down in complete despair, her head turned away from him. He had to do something.

He pulled a jellybean from the bag. "Guess what?"

She turned her head toward him, eyes closed. "What?"

He pushed the jellybean in her mouth. She chewed and swallowed. "Thanks."

He pushed another one in. Kind of like a slot machine, he thought. She'd either perk up for the win or get ever more cranky, totally wasting their only food source.

She opened her eyes. "Are you just going to feed me jellybeans all night?" she asked, sounding a little more cheerful.

He popped another one in her mouth. She chewed, swallowed, and sat up. Jellybeans for the win!

He sat next to her, offered another, and she leaned back. "I'm good, thanks," she said. "Give it a few minutes. I'm already feeling a little better."

"Should we cuddle now post-jellybean?"

She burst out laughing. He chuckled. He'd been hoping to cheer her up. Though he wouldn't mind cuddling. He was getting chilly with his hair wet and only wearing a robe.

He added a shiver for good measure. "If you haven't noticed in that warm sweater, it's getting colder in here. Sharing body heat just makes sense."

"It's not chilly. It's refreshing." She grinned. "Man up."

He recognized his own words coming back to him. He'd told her to woman up, but he'd also offered his body heat. "I'd rather woman on top."

Her deep brown eyes narrowed. "Are you for real?"

He winked. "Had to get the elephant out of the room. I know we were both thinking it."

She tried to keep a straight face but smiled again. *Win.*

"We could dance," he offered.

She sighed and held up her palms. "There's no music."

He started to sing her favorite, "SexyBack," when her hand covered his mouth.

She shook her head. "No, just no."

He took her hand, kissed the palm, and held it. She didn't pull away. "Then it seems like the obvious choice is a game."

"What kind of game?" she asked suspiciously.

His dirty hopes soared because she was at least interested enough to ask the question. "It's called getting to know each other." In his experience, confidence sharing with women always led to getting naked. He was an open book, no secrets here, but Charlotte was mysterious. Even if they didn't get naked, he was dying to know more about her. What better way to pass the time?

She held up her stop-sign hand. "No, thanks. I'm good."

He scooted closer so he could get some of her body heat, letting his leg touch hers. She allowed it. "So you'd rather sit here in the dark with one flashlight for hours, just staring at the walls?"

"I'd rather not be here at all."

"Here's how it works." He let her get the exasperated sigh out of the way before continuing. "I ask you a question and, if you get it right, you get a jellybean. If you get it wrong, you give me a kiss."

She scooted away, leaving a cold barrier of air between them. "What kind of question?"

"Any kind you want." Damn, he really was getting cold. If she wouldn't share her heat, he was going to have to get the blanket off the bed downstairs. Though he'd much rather have her on him.

"How come *you* get to decide if my answer is right or wrong?"

He scooted close again. "You can decide about my answer on your turn."

She reached for the jellybeans and he shifted them to his other side, out of her reach. If she did try to get them, she'd be stretching nicely across his lap.

She left them. "Why do you get to hold the jellybeans?"

"Because I made up the game."

"I don't want to kiss you." Her gaze dropped to his chest, where the too small robe gaped open. She licked her lips and met his eyes, desire banked there just waiting to come out and play. "I'm furious at you," she whispered.

He sensed a softening in his direction, which was awesome because he was getting harder. "No lie, I'm really getting cold after that shower and only wearing this tiny robe."

She gave him a sympathetic look. "Geez, I'm sorry, and we can't put on the heat with the engine off."

He leaned close. "Maybe you could help me out?"

"I'll get a blanket." She grabbed the flashlight and left, rushing down to the lower level.

He sat in the dark and cold and considered if he had any other moves. Not much was working on Charlotte.

She returned and covered him with a pink blanket, carefully wrapping it around his shoulders. That was kinda nice, even if it was a five-year-old-girl's blanket.

"You want some blanket?" he offered, holding it out to her. It was big enough for two.

"I'm good." She set the flashlight back on the coffee table and sat next to him, one leg crossed primly over the other.

They sat for a few minutes in silence. So…no kiss, no cuddle, no game. He was at a loss for how else to pass the time.

She broke the silence. "Tell me what you did before you were a stuntman. List all your previous jobs."

"Why? Are we playing the jellybean-kiss game?"

She ignored the kiss part of the question. "You can tell a lot about a person from what jobs they take."

"What did you do before you were a personal trainer?" he countered.

"I was in banking."

"*Braa-aa-aap*. Wrong answer. No way a fiery fierce woman like you was a conservative banker. Give me a kiss." He pointed to his cheek.

"Yes, I was, and I'd sooner slap that cheek than kiss it," she said matter-of-factly. But she didn't.

He loosened the blanket so his right arm had some leeway; then he cupped her head and placed a soft kiss on the tender spot just below her ear, giving her what she denied him. She went stock-still.

He slowly pulled away, watching her expression. Her lips parted, staring at him. It was a good look for her.

"Your turn," he said.

She shook her head and blinked a few times like he'd scrambled her brain. He was not unaffected either. He arranged the blanket better to cover a growing tent under the thin fabric of the robe.

"Like I said before," she said slowly, "what were your previous jobs?"

He ticked them off on his fingers. "Stuntman, personal trainer, and camp counselor."

"You were a camp counselor?" she asked, sounding shocked.

"You make me sound like a total beast. I was one of the oldest in a family of young'uns running hell-bent for trouble." He shifted to face her and the blanket slipped off half his body. He left it, feeling warmer now. "It was actually really great. An overnight camp for developmentally disabled kids and adults. I was like a rock star there. I did three summers before I started working full time at the gym."

Her jaw dropped.

He tipped her chin up. "What? You thought I was just an empty-hearted sex-crazed hottie?"

She nodded, smiling at him.

He smiled back.

"How'd you get involved with that?" she asked. "Did you know someone with disabilities?"

"Yeah. I was assistant coach for my dad's Little League team at the Police Athletic League. One of the kids, Teddy, had an intellectual disability. He was slow to learn, I mean really slow like he had to go to a special school. Anyway, he wasn't much good at ball, but he fucking loved the game. I coached him one-on-one before practice. He sort of really liked me. His mom asked if I'd consider being a counselor at his summer camp. It was all ages, up to age forty, with a range of developmental disabilities." He smiled a little, remembering how the campers flocked to him, and the other counselors had to work extra hard to hold their attention. "I was extremely popular," he told her. "I always figured it was because I'm a what-you-see-is-what-you-get kind of guy. I just put it all out there. Easy to understand."

She gifted him with a tender smile, squeezing his shoulder. "You have unsuspected depths. For that you get a jellybean."

"Excellent." He snagged a handful from the bag, popped

one in his mouth and offered her one. She opened her mouth and he fed it to her. She chewed, her eyes smiling at him. He fed her another and then another, and her eyes looked almost adoring gazing back at him. He might've just discovered the secret to Charlotte—she was a multiple jellybean kind of girl.

He ate a few more. "Why'd you leave New Jersey? You said you grew up there, right?"

"Yeah. Because I was tired of being with the same circle of people I grew up with. I'm one of the few people who ever left town."

"Wrong."

"What do you mean wrong?"

"Last chance to correct your answer or—" he lowered his voice to a husky growl "—I'm afraid you get a kiss."

She looked like she was considering which was worse, explaining herself or getting another kiss from him. "Where?"

He hadn't expected that answer. He leaned in, prepared to go anywhere. He spoke near her ear. "Where do you want a kiss, darlin'?"

She pointed to her cheek. He sighed, rolled his eyes, and gave her a peck.

"You're a cagey sort," he said. "Don't think I didn't notice that earlier. That's exactly why we're playing this getting-to-know-you game."

"I'm not cagey."

"Uh-huh. Your turn." He'd totally roped her into his game and now he was going to get answers. Or kisses. Either one would be satisfying.

Her eyes flashed. "Why did you take me on this boat when you didn't have the slightest idea what you were doing?"

"I wanted to impress you." He refrained from reminding her it was a map-reading error, not operator error because now her eyes were soft and full of longing. Maybe for him.

"Oh." She looked down for a moment and then met his eyes. "Why—"

"One question per turn, and I'm pretty sure I got that one right, so I get a jellybean." He popped one in his mouth and offered her one. She already had her mouth open to receive. Oh, he liked this better and better. That mouth, that pink tongue. He gave it to her, brushing his finger across her bottom lip. She chewed and gazed at him, heat in her eyes.

He went for it. "How much are you digging me on a scale of one to ten?"

She laughed. "You don't have a problem with self-confidence, do you?"

"Nope."

"Right now?"

"Yeah."

"You're about an eight. Before you were a one."

He put a hand to his heart like she'd wounded him. "What made you agree to a date if I was a one?"

She grinned cheekily. "One question per turn is what I heard."

"For real, Char. Why did you say yes?" He suddenly really needed to know. He wanted to be more than just that guy with the muscles for her.

She pressed her lips together for a moment before saying, "I admit your dance in front of my yoga class charmed me."

"Charmed you?" He'd been going for sexy.

"Yeah, it took a lot of guts. I thought he must really be interested if he's willing to risk looking like a fool in front of all those women."

He huffed and the pink blanket fell off him. "I looked like a fool?"

"No, but you could've. I had no idea which way things were going to go. I gave you a lot of points just for trying."

He felt slightly better. "So the dance boosted me a bit. How do I get to ten?"

"Why do you care so much where you stand? It's not like we're going to have a relationship. I thought this would just be a fun date. I mean, you live in LA. I live here."

"I visit regularly."

She gave him a skeptical look.

"I do. I work New York almost as much as LA. I always ask for those jobs since my family's here."

She poked him in the chest. "And what about your job? Very risky."

"Your point is?"

"You really think you're a catch?" Her lips twitched, and he realized she was messing with him. He tickled her and she shrieked. Damn, she was ticklish. He got in a good tickle by her ribs and then under her arms and her neck. She was laughing so hard she could barely swat at him. He stopped, letting her get her breath back. She wiped her eyes, still smiling a little. Her cheeks were flushed pink. He couldn't resist moving in for a quick kiss on those luscious lips.

She stared for a moment and then tilted her head up for more, her eyes closing. He obliged, cradling her head with one hand, kissing her deeply, on and on, sinking into her softness. She tasted sweet like candy and hot. So hot. Raw lust surged through him, urging him to take. He forced himself to break the kiss before he got carried away. They were both breathing hard.

He stroked her cheek with his thumb, gazing into her dark eyes. "If you gave me half a chance, I'd make the long-distance thing work." Holy crap. He shocked himself with the big R, a relationship, but then he realized with a start it was true. She was completely irresistible and he wanted a lot more than one terrible date stuck on a boat.

Her eyes widened, looking as shocked as he felt. "What're you saying?"

He dropped his hold on her, a little shaken by too much feeling too fast. This was only their first date. "Nothing. Back to the game." He scrubbed a hand over his face, not even sure why they were playing this game. Shit just got real.

"I like getting to know you," she said. "You're sweet."

He raised a brow. "Is that supposed to be a compliment? No guy wants to be sweet."

"What do you want to be?"

"Sexy for one."

"Anything else?"

He scowled because she hadn't agreed he was sexy. "Strong, confident, successful."

"Winning."

He did a double take, but she just gave him a small smile. "How am I winning?" he asked. "You were about to tear my head off when we first met. And now we're stuck in the mud—"

"Because you're being real with me and I like the real Ty."

He was speechless. She liked the real Ty, stuck in the mud on the worst date ever with no power and only jellybeans to eat? She actually saw the real Ty and liked him, not just his money or his looks or his body (all three had worked wonders for him in the past). He had no idea what to say.

And then she wrapped her arms around his neck and kissed him. And he had a very good idea what to do.

6

Charlotte knew she was playing with fire kissing Ty because the man clearly knew his way around women. One minute they were kissing hot and heavy, the next she was flat on her back, Ty between her legs, kissing along her neck. Somehow he'd shed the robe while they'd been kissing. He held his weight off her, holding himself up on his forearms, only the towel covering his lower half. The heat and size of him was delicious. Her body was on board before his lips made it past her collarbone. He yanked the cardigan open, the buttons flying who knew where, yanked the soft elastic of her peasant top down, slid the bra to the side, and sucked her nipple into his mouth. Sharp pleasure shot through her, the sensation a direct line of pleasure to her sex. She was breathless. Speech was impossible.

He lifted his head, his dark eyes burning into hers. She waited, unsure what he was going to do next. She didn't even care; she just wanted more. She grabbed his head and they slammed together again. She tasted sweetness from the jellybeans and pure erotic sin. She ran her fingers through the hair at the nape of his neck and across those amazing muscular shoulders. He nipped her bottom lip and then sucked it. Throbbing need like she'd never felt before made her spread her legs wider, inviting him in. He snagged the back of her knee and lifted her leg to wrap around him. Her other leg was trapped between him and the sofa.

He nipped along her neck, jolting her and then sucking the stinging spot. She was light-headed with the sensations flooding her body. His teeth closed over her exposed nipple and she cried out at the sharp tug of pleasure. He yanked her shirt down over her other breast, shoved the bra down, and took his fill, his tongue pushing her nipple to the roof of his mouth. She moaned, her fingernails digging into his shoulders as he rocked his pelvis against her, the friction stoking her to a fever pitch. He returned to her mouth and she kissed him frantically, out of her mind with need.

His large hand held her head from temple to jaw. "Slow down, baby."

"Ty—"

"Kissing you is like kissing fire," he said against her lips.

"Yes. I want you."

He groaned and brushed his lips against hers, the lightest touch that left her breathless, pinned under him, waiting for him to give her more.

"Please," she breathed.

He kissed her gently and her lips parted on a sigh. His tongue delved in her mouth and she slid her tongue along his, needing so much more. Her entire body hummed with need.

And then there was nothing but cold air. He stood next to the sofa, looking down at her where she lay with her breasts on display and her legs spread wide open.

She closed her eyes. "What's wrong?"

"I have never seen a more beautiful sight than you lying there like that."

She looked up at him from where he towered over her. His obvious arousal tented the towel. "I'm lying here wanting more," she said pointedly. She reached out to stroke him and he stepped sideways out of reach.

"I don't have a condom." He pulled the robe back on.

She adjusted her bra and shirt and propped up on her

elbows. "How can you not have a condom? A man like you who oozes raw sexuality should always be packing."

One corner of his mouth lifted. "I didn't want to rush things."

"Yes, you did! Nearly every word out of your mouth was sex."

He inclined his head, conceding the point. "Okay, honestly, I was so busy getting everything set up for our date that I forgot."

"Ugh!" She flopped back on the sofa, threw her arm over her eyes, and focused on the fact that they were stranded in the stinky mud in the middle of a swamp. She could feel her heartbeat in every nerve ending, even between her legs.

Ty kept explaining himself. "And I didn't realize I forgot until I was thinking about putting it on."

She sat up and studied him. He looked entirely sincere.

He explained some more. The man was a talker. "I mean, there was a lot of thought that went into tonight. The yacht, dinner, car, flowers—"

"Okay, okay!"

He stroked her hair. "You want a jellybean?"

I'd like an orgasm. "No, thanks."

He sat next to her and settled his arm around her shoulders. "Back to the getting-to-know-you game?"

"No."

"What do you wanna play?"

"I'm done playing with you."

"Don't be mad." Ty gave her shoulder a squeeze. After a moment, he said, "Do you want to know why I tried so hard to get a date with you when you were shooting me down left and right?"

That got her attention. "Yes."

His fingers trailed lightly through her hair before pulling out her hair band and running his fingers through her hair. "At first it was your beauty that caught my eye, but then I meet a lot of beautiful women."

She huffed and crossed her arms. "Gee, thanks."

He flashed a smile. "That right there is what made you stick in my mind. When you called me on my game at the wedding, you showed your strength and fierceness. I like that."

She uncrossed her arms. "Oh." Her experience was nearly the opposite. Mostly she pushed men away.

He stroked her cheek and gazed at her tenderly. "And then I saw something else."

She swallowed over the lump in her throat. "What?" she whispered.

"Just brief flashes of something more." His hand cradled her face from temple to jaw. "Underneath all that strength and beauty and fierceness, I saw a woman longing for something."

She couldn't breathe for a moment, her heart racing. "Longing for what?"

"That's what I'm hoping to find out." His thumb stroked her cheek. "The challenge, the puzzle of Charlotte."

He got her. He actually saw her vulnerable soul under all the layers of protection. No one saw that, not even her closest friends. She didn't let them see that.

"Ty," she whispered.

"Yeah."

"How did you know?"

He smirked. "You just told me."

"Ty!"

He pulled her in for a hug and spoke near her ear. "It was a hunch because…I'm the same way. Tough on the outside, tender on the inside."

She pulled back to look at him, shocked he was sharing like this. "You are?"

He nodded solemnly. "Don't tell anyone. It would ruin my rep."

No man had ever shared his most vulnerable self with her. "I won't, I swear." She gazed at him in wonder, the once arrogant cocky man transformed before her eyes into a confidant.

He kissed her briefly, gently, his mouth trailing to her neck. No urgency, only tenderness. She melted, letting herself enjoy the rare feeling of being cherished.

He pulled away much too soon. "We should stop."

"We could do other things that don't require a condom," she offered.

He dipped his head. "I'd love to help you out, but if I got you naked and I'm just in this towel and flimsy robe, well, we're bound to meet. You'll probably be begging for it, as women do, so it's just better all around if we go back to getting to know each other. It would be wa-a-ay too easy to let passion take over."

"I want passion!" she blurted way too loud.

He pulled back to stare at her, brows arched in question.

She clamped her mouth shut.

He studied her for a long moment. "Go on."

"What do you want me to say?"

"What do you want to say?"

"Forget it." She blew out a breath and turned away. "How much longer until high tide?"

"Few more hours, I figure." He snagged the jellybeans and fed her three at once. She chewed and swallowed, going from irritated to tired. She leaned back on the sofa and stared at the ceiling, frustrated with an aching need that just wouldn't quit with Ty sitting so close to her.

"Can you give me some space?" she asked.

"No." Then he reached for the jellybeans and fed her two. She chewed, and when he just ate some more, seeming unconcerned for her desperate lusty state, she shoved at him with both hands. He didn't budge. Instead he slid her a sideways glance and ate a few more jellybeans.

She shifted as far as she could get in the other direction. He closed the gap.

"I can't calm down if you're close!" she exclaimed. "My body's on full alert."

He grinned and tossed the bag on the coffee table. "That's cool. Now you know how guys feel with a blue steeler." He wrapped his arm around her shoulders and played with a lock of her hair. "I know how to fix this."

She turned to him, hopeful beyond all reason. "You do?"

"Yup. I can give you a hand job."

"A hand job," she repeated.

"It's like the guy version but for girls."

She didn't know what to say to that.

He elaborated. "Like, you know, my hand's in your pants, but you keep them on so I don't accidentally fuck you from behind."

"Accidentally?"

He cocked his head. "Is there an echo in here?"

"Couldn't you just stand in front of me for the hand job?" It occurred to her that they could fuck in either direction. His line of reasoning was peculiar.

"I guess." He flashed a smile. "Okay, fine. I admit it. I just wanted to feel your fine ass pressed against me."

She laughed and then she couldn't stop laughing.

"What's so funny?"

She shook her head. "This is quite possibly the most ridiculous conversation I've ever had."

"I'm just trying to help you out and, you know, control myself at the same time."

She waved a hand in the air. "Oh, Ty. Forget it. I'll be fine."

He gave her a sympathetic look. "But you have lady blue balls."

She lost it. He was just too funny.

He huffed. "If you're going to laugh, forget it."

She tried to stop, but one look at his disgruntled expression had her cracking up. She might be losing her mind.

He tickled her in retaliation. She shrieked with laughter and tried to wiggle away when his arms closed around her suddenly, holding her tight in his embrace. He kissed her temple before dipping his head, his mouth grazing her ear as he spoke in a husky tone. "I'm glad I'm stuck here with you."

Her heart thumped furiously. Something about Ty's open sincerity got to her.

His warm eyes met hers. She nearly sighed. "Oh," was all she could manage before his mouth covered hers. She fell into a dizzying hungry feeling of pure heat and open need.

He dropped his forehead to hers. "What're you doing to me?"

"Nothing. I—"

He silenced her with another kiss before saying, "I have an idea. Let me see if Will left any condoms in the bedroom."

"Why didn't you do that before?"

He grimaced. "Because he got snipped after the twins were born last year. It's only a remote possibility that there's some leftovers lying around."

"Leftovers that are more than a year old?"

"They don't go bad."

"Of course they do. Haven't you seen the expiration date on the box?"

He smirked. "Never had to worry about that."

"Just how many do you go through in a month?"

"Hold that thought," he said, snagging the flashlight. The room went pitch black.

She stood and grabbed his arm. "Wait. I'll go with you. The bed sounds better than the sofa."

He led her back to the sofa and pushed her down by the shoulder. "Bed is not going to work. Not if there's no condoms. I want you too damn much and, for certain, you're going to be begging me for more."

She snort-laughed. "I've never begged in my life."

He raised his brows. "You will."

Her breath caught at his certainty. Before she could come up with some snappy reply, he smirked, turned, and headed for the stairs.

She flopped back on the sofa, wound tight. Long minutes passed. Obviously he couldn't find any. *Fine.* She crossed to the window and looked out to the park. There were some streetlights on. A group of guys were hanging out, sitting on some boulders.

She yelped as Ty swatted her butt. She whirled and smacked his arm. "You scared me." He'd set the flashlight back on the coffee table, making the room glow with dim light.

His arms wrapped around her. "Stealthy for my size, aren't I? No condoms."

"That's okay. I'm not in the mood."

"Bummer," he said, his hand sliding between her legs. "You sure? Because I'm feeling a lot of heat down here."

Her knees wobbled. That never happened to her.

His fingers pressed into her and she whimpered, hanging onto his arms for balance. "I think I feel a pulse," he said. "That is one powerful need. You want the hand job?"

She had to tell him. Just as soon as she could catch her breath.

He pulled his hand away. "What's wrong?"

The words seemed to be stuck in her throat.

"What?" he pressed.

She looked at a point over his shoulder. Was she really going to admit this to the man who oozed sexual confidence?

He took a step back. "I got it. Too much, too fast. No prob—"

"It's not that," she blurted.

His arms wrapped around her again and she nearly sagged in relief. His mouth trailed to her ear. "Whisper it to me."

She took a deep breath, went up on her tiptoes, and confessed, "I haven't had an orgasm with a partner in three years."

7

———

Charlotte held her breath. He'd probably think she was the problem. Like she was too closed off to enjoy sex. Maybe she shouldn't have said anything.

He straightened, pulling back to stare at her. "Ouch. That's terrible."

Heat flooded her cheeks. "Forget it."

He pushed the hair from her face, tucking it behind her ear. "You can't say something like that and expect me to forget it. That's like waving a flag."

"What kind of flag?" She wasn't trying to give him an SOS call of desperation. Wait, was she?

One corner of his mouth lifted in a small smile. That might've bothered her, smiling in the face of her embarrassment, but his eyes were warm and full of understanding, and he spoke in a gentle tone. "It's a *help me out, Ty,* flag and also a warning—sex doesn't work for me, so you might as well know that ahead of time."

Damn, he was insightful. She'd been hoping he'd help her out yet feared he'd be disappointed in the end. Still, this conversation was beyond awkward. She tried to pull away, but his arm banded around her waist, holding her tight. She could feel his erection pressing into her belly. At least she hadn't completely turned him off.

He tipped her chin up to look at him. "What kind of men are you dating?"

"Jerks apparently."

A flash of sudden understanding crossed his features. "And you thought I'd be a jerk too, so you could dismiss me, but then it turned out you *liked* me." He smiled widely at this last part. She didn't give him the words, even though she did like him a lot, because it was clear he already knew.

He wound her long hair around his fist and went on. "You must know by now I love a challenge."

She swallowed as he tugged her hair, tilting her head up. "It's not a challenge," she whispered.

"What is it, then?" His lips grazed hers. "An invitation?"

She flushed, embarrassed by the conversation. She never should've brought up her crappy sex life. "Let's not talk about it."

He kissed her, hot and wet and deep. She whimpered in the back of her throat, eager for more, gripping his large shoulders, longing to feel the heat and weight of him on her. He broke the kiss and dipped his head to her ear. "So the guys don't know what they're doing or you're just not getting hot for them because they're all jerks?"

"Both," she admitted.

"That won't be a problem with me." His hand slid between her legs. "You're already hot for me and, trust me, baby, I know what I'm doing. You want the hand job?"

"Yes," she replied immediately.

"I could go down on you," he offered. "But then you're going to have to get dressed *immediately* after because I know you're going to beg me to fuck you after that."

"Yes." Whatever it was, yes, yes, yes.

He released her hair and cradled her jaw. "You are so beautiful."

"Stop talking."

"So bossy too."

"Ty!"

His hand moved from between her legs and stroked her shoulder instead. "That's probably your problem right there."

"You're my problem right now."

"Guys don't like to be bossed."

"Ty, I swear—" His mouth covered hers, kissing her long and deep. The man was so good at that. She threw her arms around his neck, pressing her entire body against his hard planes, aching to get closer. As close as two people could get.

He broke the kiss suddenly and scooped her up, cradled in his arms. He crossed to the flashlight. "Grab that. We're heading downstairs." He tilted her toward the coffee table and she shrieked at the sudden dip. "Grab it," he ordered.

She snagged the flashlight and he yanked her back up safe in his arms. She lit the way as he headed toward the stairs. "I thought you couldn't control yourself in a bed."

"Now who's talking too much?"

She got quiet because the less talking the better as far as sex was concerned. She didn't want to overanalyze it, she wanted to *feel*. She sensed he could give her what had eluded her for so long.

"There's mirrors on the wall of the master bedroom," he said. "I thought you'd like to watch your first orgasm in three years."

She shook her head. "I don't want to look at myself. I want to look at your amazing body." She stroked his arm, shoulder to bicep, in appreciation.

"Of course all women want that," he said matter-of-factly, "but since I'm the one not getting any, this goes down the way I say."

Now who's bossy? She kept the thought to herself because if he could actually give her an orgasm, he could go ahead and do things his way. He set her down at the top of the stairs and she led the way down with the flashlight.

"I could always give you a return hand job," she offered.

"We'll see after you get yours."

"I don't think I've ever talked quite so much about my orgasm with a man before."

"Yeah, I put it all out there. I told ya what you see is what you get with me. No secrets."

She swallowed, having more than her share of secrets.

They reached the master bedroom and Ty snagged the flashlight from her hands and set it on the floor near the wall of mirrors. He tried a few different spots for it at different angles until he was satisfied.

He took off his robe, tossing it to the side, and tied the towel tighter around his waist. "That's as secure as I can make it. Take off your shirt and bra."

"You take it off."

He ignored her request, busying himself running his fingers through her hair. "Then turn around, cup your breasts, and look at how beautiful you are."

She blinked rapidly, eyes hot. She didn't feel beautiful and she definitely didn't want to look at herself. She wanted to look at him. Years of emotional eating had given her a love-hate relationship with her body. Not to mention all her other health problems. She knew she was fit and toned now. But that fact never sank in deep enough to where she felt good about her body. Accomplished, yes, but not good.

Ty took over, stripping her sweater and shirt off, tossing them over his shoulder, and undoing the bra with one quick movement before sliding it off and tossing it too. He turned her to the mirror, cupping her breasts with his large hands, holding them so his fingers scissored her nipples tightly. The intense pleasure won over her initial reluctance. She watched as he kissed along her neck and up to her ear, his hot breath fanning over the sensitive shell of her ear. "See? So beautiful."

He massaged and stroked her breasts, making her moan. She leaned back and melted against his heat, her head resting on his shoulder. His hand slid straight down her stomach to the button of her pants. He spoke in her ear. "Now we're getting into dangerous territory. No matter how good this feels, don't beg me to fuck you. We'll get to that on our second date with protection."

She smiled. It was almost funny, his assurance of her begging. On top of that, his complete confidence of a second date, of guaranteed sex on that date.

He cupped her firmly between the legs and she lost her smile. "Got it?" he prompted.

"Yes," she breathed.

He grunted and reached both hands around to unbutton and unzip her pants. He pushed them down, pulling her bikini panties with them, and helped her out of them, leaving her high-heeled sandals on. He stood and slid his fingers unerringly to pleasure central. She bucked against his hand.

"So sensitive," he rasped in her ear. She wasn't normally; she suspected it was all Ty. "Let's see what you like."

His fingers were wicked, stroking up and down her, swirling, pinching, watching her responses in the mirror. Everything he did felt amazing. He slid his fingers inside her, stroking on the inside, and her knees buckled.

"Oh yeah," he rumbled in her ear, "I got you now." He kept it up, his fingers stroking deep inside her, and then he shifted the heel of his hand, pressing firmly on the one spot most men couldn't seem to find. Idiots.

She panted, eyes closed, the sensations overwhelming her. "You're a genius."

He chuckled low in her ear. "Watch. You're so wet. You're going to go off so hard."

"I'm close," she said on a gasp.

"Watch."

She shook her head.

His hand stilled, holding her in firm possession. "You have to surrender to it. I'll get you close and pull you back as many times as that takes."

"Ty," she moaned.

"You'll come a lot more when you trust me to get you there."

"I do."

"Then watch. I want you to see who's giving it to you and how amazingly sexy you look when you surrender to pleasure."

She throbbed at the words. Ty groaned and pressed his erection against her ass. "This is what you do to me, sexy woman. But I won't be satisfied until you are."

She opened her eyes to watch, expecting to be brought down from the height she'd started to climb, but Ty's gaze in the mirror was intense. He slid a large hand across her chest to cup her breast and did another wicked stroke on her tender sex. She let out a shaky breath.

"Good," he crooned in her ear. "I got you. You're not going anywhere until I'm done with you."

She tensed, suddenly feeling trapped with his large body pressing at her back, his hand dominating her sex, his arm across her chest. She tried to move and realized she couldn't. Her heartbeat thrummed in her ears.

"Easy," he said, but his touch was anything but as he pressed her for more, stroking faster and harder, and then leaning down to her neck to suck the tender flesh. Her surrender was shockingly immediate, her entire body softening, her vision dimming to just the beautiful sight of Ty giving and her receiving. She trembled on the brink of the orgasm that had eluded her for so long. He pulled his hand away from where she desperately needed it and tilted her head back for a kiss.

"I'm so close," she said urgently.

He gave her a wicked smile. "I know. Look at how turned on you are."

She groaned and met his eyes in the mirror, getting irritated with him.

"Relax," he said, stroking her lazily. "We've got hours."

She opened her mouth to protest when he suddenly lifted her, carrying her to the bed. He set her in the center on a cool sheet and then snagged the flashlight, setting it on the nightstand.

"I thought you couldn't control yourself in a bed," she said.

He pushed her legs apart and slid his hands under her bottom, lifting her. His words ran hot over her tender sex. "I've got to get a taste of sweet Charlotte." He gazed into her eyes as he took one long taste. She jerked and then melted, her body surrendering to the intensity of Ty.

His mouth was magic. Nothing had ever felt this good. Her fingers fisted in the sheets as she moved mindlessly against him. Small cries and gasps escaped as he took her higher and higher and then eased her back, letting her know he controlled her pleasure. Something in her snapped, some last bit of tension straining for release, and then she was lost in a haze of white-hot pleasure. Everything narrowed down to Ty's all-consuming touch as he held her to his pace, sometimes a hard rush of pleasure, sometimes an easy roll, but always, always she trusted him to give her exactly what she needed when she needed it. He hummed against her and then sucked hard. She cried out as the orgasm slammed through her. Shock waves of pleasure radiated from her core and Ty stayed with her as the pleasure sparked on endlessly.

Finally, she felt him shift away and she let out a long sigh of pure bliss.

"That was amazing," he said.

She murmured agreement.

He climbed up her body and kissed her; then he dropped to her side and pulled her into his arms, chest to chest, his erection pressing into her belly, his leg wedging between hers.

"You're amazing," she murmured.

"I know."

She ran her hand down his chest toward his erection. "Your turn."

He stilled her hand. "I'm not done with you."

"N-no." She bit her lip. "That was…I've never come that hard in my life. There's no way I can do it again."

"Of course you can. You're a multiple orgasm kind of girl."

Actually that had never happened. "How do you know that?"

He stroked her hair. "You're a multiple jellybean kind of girl."

"And that means…?"

"You naturally enjoy a lot of a good thing."

A surge of affection ran through her. She wrapped her arms around his middle and squeezed him tight.

He cupped her head, his voice rumbling through his chest. "I hope you know we're having a second date and a third and a fourth—"

She interrupted, even though some part of her loved the sweet sentiment. "Let's just take it one day at a time."

His fingers tangled in her hair, tilting her head back and then skimming kisses gently down her throat, his stubble scraping against the sensitive skin. His tongue dipped between her collarbones before he returned to her mouth, kissing both corners of it. Her lips parted on a sigh. He sucked her lower lip. "You really think any other guy can do what I just did?"

She smiled. "You certainly don't have any confidence issues."

"You're the one who said I was amazing, and did I hear correctly? A genius?" He grinned, rolled to his back and hauled her on top of him. He arranged her, spreading her legs so she was cupping his erection over the towel. "You might be the first person to ever say that."

She wiggled against him. "Let me help you out."

He palmed her ass, stilling her movements. "Tell me a secret, mysterious Charlotte."

She dropped her head to his chest, listening to the solid thump of his heart, her own heart pounding. He stroked her hair, waiting patiently.

She took a deep breath and lifted her head. "Why do you think I'm mysterious?"

He chucked her under the chin. "Because I sense that while I'm all *what you see is what you get*, you're all *deep secrets that shall never be revealed*. Come on, you told me your no-orgasm secret. Don't you feel better now?"

She dropped her head to his chest again. "I don't have any deep secrets."

He trailed his fingers down her spine, giving her shivers. "We've got hours to play the secret game."

"There are no secrets," she insisted.

"Next orgasm is contingent upon a secret reveal," he said casually.

She jerked her head up. "Ty! I told you there's no secrets."

"You're an assassin."

"No!"

"Your parents were assassins."

"Nobody was assassinating anybody!"

She rolled off him and he followed, trapping her under him. He gazed down at her with a slow grin. "Pretty damn touchy for someone who isn't an assassin." He shifted, kissing the tender spot under her ear. Warm sensation relaxed her as he worked his way down and then kissed along her shoulder. He shifted lower, cupping her breast and flicking his tongue across her nipple. It tightened into a hard peak. "Nice," he murmured before scraping his teeth against it. She moaned. His tongue flicked again, playing with her, and then he kissed along the side of her breast. Her fingers tangled in his hair, surrendering to pleasure.

"Tell me something I don't know about you," he urged between soft kisses round and round the aching peak.

"I'm from New Jersey," she managed.

"I know that. What else?" He teased her with his tongue, and then he slid his weight to her side, his other hand sliding over to play with her other breast. The aching need spiked when he sucked her nipple hard just as his hand slid between her legs, stroking in lazy circles. She panted; there was just nothing she wanted more in that moment than Ty inside her.

"Ty, fuck me."

He ignored her, shifting to suckle her other breast, his fingers thrusting inside her.

She moaned, achy and needing more. "I can't get pregnant. It's okay."

He released her breast and stared at her. "Are you on the pill?"

She closed her eyes against the familiar sting. "It doesn't matter."

"Of course it matters."

Her throat felt tight. "Just fuck me."

"Charlotte, baby, are you okay?"

And then like a complete idiot, she started to cry.

8

———

Ty swallowed, his own throat tight in sympathy with Charlotte's tears. He tucked her into his arms, throwing his leg over hers and holding her head against his chest so she'd feel surrounded by the hug. Her shoulders shook with sobs.

He should've kept his big mouth shut.

It was just that she'd been so cagey in answering his getting-to-know-you questions and it had made him curious. Most women blabbed more than he ever wanted to know. Now he was filled with remorse. Secrets were that way for a reason.

After a while, she was just sniffling, seeming to be out of tears.

"Sorry," he said. "I didn't mean to make you cry."

"I don't even know why I'm crying. It's stupid."

He stroked her hair. "It's not stupid. It's a whopper you've been hanging onto."

She lifted her head and looked at him. He could just make out her shiny eyes in the glow of the flashlight. Killed him.

"You want to know my secret?" she whispered.

There was more? He thought her not being able to get pregnant was the big secret.

He pushed her hair back from her face. "Only if you want to tell me."

She took a shaky breath. "I'm only telling you this because I cried all over you. And maybe this will send you running for the hills, but I don't expect some rosy future, so what the hell."

"Whatever you have to say isn't going to send me running. I told you I want to see you again after this."

She shook her head. "You won't."

"Try me."

"I'm thirty-one—"

"Big deal. So am I."

"That's not the secret."

"Oh."

She rubbed his chest absently. "I'm thirty-one and I'm running out of time to have a baby."

"I thought you couldn't."

"My chances of conceiving naturally are really small, like one percent. I had severe endometriosis; it left a lot of scar tissue in my uterus, extremely painful. The doctor removed it surgically a couple of months ago and then she told me when I was ready I should consider in vitro, but not to wait too long because even that would be more difficult the older I got." She sucked in a deep breath, and he remained utterly still. "So now I'm thinking of blowing all my savings on in vitro with a sperm donor before I run out of time."

He was having trouble thinking clearly with all this stunning information. "So you're on the pill, or you're not on the pill?" he blurted.

"That's not the point!"

"Okay. What is the point?"

She blew out a long breath. "I'm not on it because I'm thinking of in vitro. Once I'm back on the pill, it'll take months to be fertile again." She got quiet and in the stillness of that moment he realized the longing he'd sensed in Charlotte was not for a partner to love, as he'd hoped, but for a baby to love.

"You still have a one percent chance," he said. "Or you could adopt."

She put a hand on his cheek and he held it there. "I

haven't told anyone this. I guess because it was so hard to explain why I'd want a baby with my genes and being single. I just feel like it's something I have to do before it's too late."

So, basically, he was in bed with a woman looking for a settled-down future with kids, with or without a man. Why did she confide in him? Not her family, not her closest friends. Was it because she planned to never see him again? Or was hoping he'd run for the hills? He was the furthest thing from. He was experienced enough to know when that rare connection happened between two people.

"I'm an idiot," she said.

He tugged her hair. "Don't talk about yourself like that. You're great. Of course you'd want a baby with your genes. You're gorgeous and smart and sweet."

She was quiet for a long moment, and he gave her the time to let that compliment sink in. Finally, she spoke, her tone serious. "What happens on the boat stays on the boat."

He tried to lighten the mood. "I'd love to help you out, but we've only had one date. You know I'd be that lucky one percent that plants a seed in there."

She didn't crack a smile. "Turn off the flashlight. And when it comes back on, we *never* speak of what happens in the dark again."

"Oh-kay," he said slowly, unsure what she had in mind. It didn't feel like a hot and sexy moment, but he was game if she was.

He snagged the flashlight and turned it off. The darkness was so complete it was like he'd closed his eyes. He eased back to her, not wanting to elbow her accidentally. He felt warm satiny skin and tucked her back in his arms, throwing his leg over her for good measure. And then she shocked him, tossing out secrets in rapid succession:

"My genes suck.

"My dad is in jail.

"My mom was a stripper.

"I've been on my own since I was sixteen.

"I had a sugar daddy in college to pay my tuition.

"I used to be morbidly obese.

"And it's been more than three years since I had an orgasm with a partner because the men I date are jerks or morons or, I don't know, maybe I just hate men."

His jaw dropped. He felt like he'd jumped through a plate-glass window, only it wasn't the showbiz kind, it was real. Stinging needles of pain everywhere, her pain, that he felt in sympathy.

A beat passed in silence. He heard her take a deep breath.

"Anything else?" he asked.

"That's all I can think of," she said softly. "You can see why I wanted to leave Jersey for a fresh start. Everyone knew my history."

"Why were you on your own at sixteen?"

"I was tired of the parade of men in our apartment. It was just me and my mom. I had a deadbolt on my bedroom door and a knife in my nightstand drawer."

He hissed out a breath, instinctively holding her tighter. "Did any of those men touch you?"

"No, but there were some close calls. I didn't feel safe. My mom was drunk most of the time." She blew out a breath. "So I came up with a plan to graduate high school a year early, the guidance counselor helped me arrange it, and I worked as a babysitter for a nice woman, Myrna, who lived near my school. Eventually I moved into Myrna's basement, helping around the house and taking care of her young kids in exchange for room and board. Then I graduated, got a cheap apartment near Rutgers, that's the state school of New Jersey, so I paid in-state tuition. I worked full time and went to college part time year-round, except for one year of full-time college with the help of my sugar daddy. I wasn't the only one doing that, a friend told me about it. A lot of girls were signing up through this website as a way to get out of college debt-free."

He tensed, imagining young Charlotte with no one looking out for her. His own baby sister was well protected by him and his brothers and their cop dad. "Did you sleep with your sugar daddy?"

"No, he was an elderly man that just wanted company

from a young college girl. I went to dinner and theater with him, read him the newspaper, stuff like that. He paid my tuition, but then I dropped out because I couldn't bear looking at myself in the mirror. It was a little too close to the way my mom was with a variety of men from the strip club."

He stroked her silky hair. And here he was making her look at herself in the mirror. But she had warmed to it. The trust she placed in him overwhelmed him.

She took a shuddering breath. "After that ended, I went back to college part time, working my way through. Had a few good years in banking, that's how I could afford my house, and then I guess I just burned out. I lost myself and then I moved, got fit, made new friends, and eventually found a new career."

"That's good."

"Yeah, it is good. I'm working hard not to let my issues define me, but…I guess they still affect me. I have a hard time opening up. Relationships are tough for me." She sighed. "And now with me running out of time on my baby window…I don't know about my future. I have a lot of hard decisions to make."

He could read between the lines. She was letting him know she didn't see a relationship for them in the future. His chest ached at the thought of this being all they had, one date stuck in the mud. But she had opened up to him, emotionally and physically. That had to mean something.

"Everyone has something wrong with them," he said. "Objectively speaking, you're amazing."

"You're not objective at all. You just have blue balls."

He chuckled. "Maybe I do, but it's still true. You turned out amazing despite whatever your parents did. Look at you with a great career that you love, great friends, I mean, you've got that group of ladies from smutty book club—"

"Happy Endings Book Club."

"And you own your own home. By any measure, you're a success."

Her arms squeezed tight around his middle and she buried her head in his chest.

"It's true," he said, cupping her head. She lifted her head and he gave her a tender kiss. A surge of affection shot through him for all she'd been through and all she'd overcome. She was exactly the kind of woman he respected—kickass and strong. He broke the kiss and stroked her cheek, feeling all kinds of mushy where she was concerned. Then he had a scary thought about her dad in jail. "Is your dad violent?"

She blew out a breath. "No. He went to one of those cushy white-collar jails for fraud. He was a financial advisor and took people's money, funneling it into his own accounts. I didn't even know him that well. I saw him like twice a year."

At least she hadn't had to deal with a violent man at home. "I had the opposite. A fantastic dad and a mom that bailed on her six kids. I haven't seen her since I was six years old."

"I'm sorry."

"The worst part is she showed up recently back home to make amends or whatever and I missed it."

"Maybe you could look her up."

"Josh says not to bother. He's probably right. It was too little too late. I guess it just bugged me that she didn't ask about me or call or anything since she was getting back in touch with everyone."

"That sucks," she said.

"Yup." He wrapped her long hair around his fist, loving the feel of it in his hand. "Bet you're wondering what's wrong with me."

"I thought it was your mom bailing."

"Nope. You might find this hard to believe—" he lowered his voice "—but some people say I have a big head."

She bumped his jaw and then slid her hands all over his head. "Feels normal to me."

"I meant a little too confident."

She laughed. "I know. I was joking and you do have an abundance of confidence. It can be a bit much sometimes, bordering on arrogant."

"I gotta be amped up with confidence for my job. If you

have even a moment's hesitation or doubt, a stunt can go south fast. Mind and body are tightly tied together."

"Your job scares me."

He found himself smiling both because she cared enough to be scared for him and because he loved the thrill of his job. "I love it." He stroked a finger down the soft skin of her neck. "You're being real with me and I like the real Charlotte."

"I like the real Ty too," she said softly.

He kissed her again, gently, hoping to ease her pain.

"None of that leaves this room."

"It's locked in the vault," he said.

"I like you better than any man I've ever met in my entire life."

His eyes stung. Jesus. This woman had a way of squeezing his heart. "Thank you." He needed to look her in the eye. He eased away from her and turned on the light, aiming it toward her for a good look. Her nose was red, her cheeks tearstained.

She blinked a few times. "Why'd you turn on the light?"

He left the light facing up for a dim glow and pulled her back in his arms. "I needed to see the brave woman who shared so much."

She spoke to his chest. "We agreed never to talk about it once the light was on."

"Charlotte," he said slowly, searching for the right words to express how much all of that meant to him, "thank you for trusting me with your secrets, with the mirror, with your orgasm." Red dotted her cheeks at that last part. "I promise to always take care of whatever you gift me with."

"It's hardly a gift."

He stroked her hair and kissed her. "It is."

She sighed. "I'm so tired."

"Course you are. I didn't feed you anything but jellybeans, gave your body a workout, and you just unloaded everything that's been weighing you down. I'd say you feel like a balloon that lost all its air, but later you'll soar even higher because of it." He chuckled. "That sounded so deep. I guess it's all that secret sharing kind of touched a deeper place. Most of my first dates don't go like this at all."

She was quiet. He looked down to see she'd fallen asleep.

He stroked her soft hair, wondering at the strength she must've had to pull herself up from where she came from and have the life she wanted on her terms. It bothered him that she was thinking about having a baby on her own because it meant she didn't think any man would ever step up and want to have a family with her. Some part of him wanted to be that man, even as the more rational part of him said that was crazy. Just because he stepped into Charlotte's life while she was at this crossroads didn't mean he was there too. Yes, he lived for the rush, but not in relationships. *Wake up. She spelled it out in big bold letters. She's not looking for a relationship. She doesn't see a future with you.*

He must've drifted off because the next thing he knew, a bullhorn was blaring. He rolled away from Charlotte and sat up, disoriented. "Shit. What time is it?"

Charlotte pushed her hair out of her face. "Huh?"

It was still dark. It must be the police coming to rescue them. "Get dressed," he told her. "It must be high tide."

He fixed the towel around his waist, snagged the robe, and made his way upstairs. A spotlight panned over the deck from a nearby police boat. Damn, it was cold. He tied the robe tight around his waist and shoved his feet into his muddy sneakers.

"NYPD," a voice boomed through a megaphone. "Pick up your radio for an update."

He raised a hand. "Got it!" He headed to the main control panel, snagged the radio, and pressed the button. "Is it high tide?"

There was a staticky noise like a long put-upon sigh. "Yes. We're sending George out to steer you out of the mud. Prepare to help him on board."

"Roger, over," he said, wondering exactly how he was supposed to do that. He headed out on the back deck, where there was a ladder to climb on board.

"Saved," Charlotte said from behind him. He turned to find her fully dressed. For some reason that made her seem closed off and distant, or maybe that was just her expression. *What happens on the boat stays on the boat.* Their time together was done.

He worked for his normal upbeat tone. "They're sending a guy out and then I'm going to help him board."

"You should probably get that pole with the hook on the end."

That's what the pole's for? "Sure. That was what I was thinking."

She crossed her arms against the cold, looking over at the police boat. He retrieved the pole and watched as a rowboat was lowered into the water.

"This has been the craziest first date I've ever been on," she said, staring at the man rowing over to them in a wet suit.

"This has been the *best* first date I've ever been on," he replied. It was true and he didn't bother to hide it, used to speaking his mind. Except for the small embarrassment over getting the boat stuck, he'd enjoyed every moment with her. There had been no awkwardness, no boredom, just fun and then so much more than he'd ever expected. No one had ever opened up to him like that before. It touched him deeply.

She met his eyes, tried to smile but couldn't quite manage it.

He swallowed over the lump in his throat.

Her voice came out like forced cheer. "You can't beat being stuck in the mud and stranded for half the night."

"No, you can't," he murmured.

She turned away, watching the man row to them for a moment. "I'm going to get those jellybeans," she said and slipped inside the cabin.

And then George, a grizzly old man with wild gray hair, was hollering from his rowboat for Ty to throw him a line. Ty looked around. No rope anywhere that he could see. He leaned over with the pole instead.

"Seriously, man?" George asked. "No wonder you're stuck

in the damn mud." He ignored the pole and simply stepped out of his boat and into the swampy water. Then he swam and, when he couldn't swim anymore, waded through the thick mud. He boarded the boat on his own from the ladder.

"Sorry I couldn't help more," Ty said.

George shook his head. "You don't belong with a beauty like this."

For a moment Ty thought he meant Charlotte, but then George kept grumbling about her fine lines and some kind of engine he didn't even know the yacht had before spraying himself with a hose Ty hadn't noticed before. There wasn't much water before it petered out.

The rest was a crazy big deal as George worked to get the yacht unstuck, which, even with his expertise, was no easy task. By the time they were safely back to the dock, Charlotte was withdrawn and way too quiet. Ty told himself to leave things as they were, just take her home and say goodbye. But some part of him rebelled. He wanted to keep hanging out with her. Just a little longer, a little more fun before she moved on with her big decisions and future that was never supposed to include him.

"You want to stop for a bite?" he asked her. It was nearly two a.m. and he knew she must be starving.

"No, thanks. Just take me home."

He did. She slept on the drive home, or at least she pretended to sleep, because the moment he pulled into her driveway, she grabbed her purse, said a quick thanks, and left. He turned off the car and got out to walk her to the door, but she slipped inside before he even got a chance. The sinking feeling in his gut told him she wouldn't even consider a casual second date. No stripper-style dance was going to work magic for him this time. *Oh shit.* Her mom had been a stripper. Somehow he'd triggered nearly every hot-button issue with her. He couldn't blame her if she never wanted to see him again.

He got back in the car, turned it on, and just sat there staring at her front door, his throat tight, his chest aching like he'd lost something important. The only reason he felt this intense...longing was because of the unusual circumstances of their date. Hell, anyone would bond over being stranded somewhere together.

He shifted the car in reverse and shot out of her driveway, needing to put some serious distance between them.

9

Charlotte stretched out her legs in her comfy oversized tunic and leggings in her seat at the Happy Endings Book Club meeting on Thursday night and mentally prepared how she would answer her friends when they asked about her date with Ty. Her plan was to keep her mouth shut at the meeting so as not to draw attention to herself, but she didn't know how long that would pass muster. The club had originally begun as a singles book club, so they always took a keen interest in each other's love lives.

The ladies were getting cups of the amazing coffee served at their regular meeting place in Clover Park, Something's Brewing Café. Charlotte had brought her own large travel cup of green tea for the antioxidants. She fiddled with her cell phone, trying to hold off any curious questions. Her friends had witnessed her and Ty's first fiery meeting at the wedding and second fiery meeting at Garner's. They also knew about his Magic Mike-style dance. Who could resist sharing that juicy bit? She only wished she'd had the foresight to video it for them because it was *amazing*. But now, though there was comedy to be had in their disastrous sunset dinner cruise, what followed in the dark was not something she was prepared to share. In fact, she deeply regretted blurting out all her painful secrets. Not even her friends knew that stuff.

She tucked her cell phone away, suddenly depressed. Her friends, all in their twenties, sat in the circle of chairs around her, chattering happily, and all Charlotte could think was she'd never feel that carefree again. Something had irrevocably changed for her on that boat. Saying everything out loud gave it power and now she had to deal with the consequences. She had to make some hard decisions, go back on the pill or not, try in vitro before it was too late, or live with the fact that she'd voluntarily missed her window.

Ty could never be a serious consideration in those decisions. Even if they worked out the long-distance thing, he was a stuntman risking his life on a regular basis. It was far easier to go into motherhood with the expectation of going it alone. A stuntman for her baby's father? Her stomach rolled just thinking about it. What if he died on her?

Hailey interrupted her dark thoughts, taking her seat in the circle of women. "So today I've got a new kind of romance, paranormal, which means there's some magic!"

"Like Harry Potter?" Mad shook her head, her fire-engine red hair long enough now to get in her face with the movement. She shoved her hair back. "Not gonna cut it. I need real hot scenes. Now that I've got Park, I've got someone to do them with."

Hailey waved that away. "It's got hot scenes. A sexy vampire with a huge, um, *you know*." She flushed bright pink.

"Cock," Mad supplied helpfully.

Hailey flicked her strawberry blonde hair over her shoulder. "Yes, well, it's very sexy."

"You like a guy who's extra large?" Lauren asked, crinkling her nose. She was a very sweet second grade teacher. "That seems uncomfortable."

"You just need to be properly worked over to take him," Mad replied matter-of-factly. She looked around for confirmation and, receiving none, added, "Park's hung."

Charlotte bit back a snarky remark. Mad would *not* shut up about the fabulous, romantic, sexy, hung Park. Of course, they were all happy for her, thrilled at her engagement, but it was getting to be a bit *in your face*. Ty was hung, too, not that she got to experience—shit. She was getting turned on thinking about him. *No, no, no.* Not going there. She wasn't even sure she could look him in the eye again with all he knew about her. It was even hard to look his sister, Mad, in the eye now, even as well as Charlotte knew and loved Mad because she could see the resemblance in the dark brown eyes and around the mouth, which was weird because of what Ty's mouth had done for her.

Hailey cleared her throat. "Anyway, it's called *Accidentally Married to a Vampire.*"

"Accidentally?" Charlotte asked.

The women tittered.

"Julia highly recommended it." Hailey stared them all down, challenging any of them to contradict Julia. That was a former book club member and internationally bestselling author of the Fierce trilogy, the book that had first brought them all together. "She also recommended *Carnal Werewolf,* but I wasn't sure about the furry love angle."

The women debated spiritedly over fangs versus fur and finally concluded fangs were sexier.

Hailey clapped once. "Okay then, I will get us started on chapter one. But first, Charlotte, how did it go on your sunset dinner cruise?"

Charlotte froze, surprised at the sudden turn in conversation despite trying to prepare for it. The women turned to her as one. The group had expanded recently, so that was a lot of eyes on her. The original group—Hailey, Mad, Lauren, Ally, and Carrie—plus newcomers Missy, Lexi, and Sabrina.

Mad piped up. "I can't believe Ty pulled off a dance like that! Damn, I wish I had seen it."

"And he really did a backflip?" Hailey asked.

"Oh, he's been doing backflips for years," Mad said. "It's mostly in your core muscles. Haven't seen him dance much, though."

Charlotte grinned. "He was amazing! So you can see why I found it hard to resist his invitation. I mean, he danced in front of all the women in my yoga class."

The women sighed. "So romantic," someone murmured.

She hadn't really thought it romantic so much as supremely sexy. Maybe it was kind of romantic.

"Maybe he could teach Park some moves," Mad said thoughtfully.

Charlotte resisted an eye roll. *Let the woman enjoy her mushy love.*

"So how was the date?" Hailey pressed. "Are you going to see him again?"

Charlotte focused on the first question. "Pretty much a disaster. Turns out he borrowed the yacht, had no idea how to read the freaking map, and we ended up stranded in the mud, waiting for high tide so the NYPD could rescue us."

The women gasped.

"You had to be rescued?" someone asked.

"You were stranded with that hottie?" Ally asked. "What happened?" She waggled her brows, which disappeared under her blonde bangs.

"Nothing happened," Charlotte lied. "He was a gentleman." Only a gentleman would've given her such a fantastic orgasm and then asked for nothing in return.

"Bummer," Mad said. "Sorry. My dad drummed the gentleman thing into all my brothers. I didn't think it took with Ty that much. He usually does whatever the hell he wants."

Charlotte took a long drink of green tea, working on toning down the heat she could feel creeping up her neck. "Anyway, since we were stuck in deep mud, we had to cut the engine, which meant the sunset dinner cruise had no dinner. He couldn't cook the spaghetti—"

"Spaghetti, ha!" Mad exclaimed. "I knew he couldn't cook a real dinner."

"He had good intentions," Charlotte snapped. She took a deep calming breath. "The spaghetti sauce was frozen, so we couldn't eat that." She stopped for a moment, barely registering the murmurs of sympathy, as she realized she'd forgotten all about the sauce once things had started heating up with Ty. It was unusual, her response to him, even thinking about him gave her a hot flash. Some part of her wished they'd had a chance to have a little more naked fun time. She never did get to—

"Let me guess," Mad said, "you crunched raw spaghetti for dinner."

Charlotte quickly wrapped up her story, not wanting to dwell on Ty and her unusually lusty thoughts. "We found some jellybeans. I have hypoglycemia, so it made me feel really tired with the sugar highs and lows. I even took a nap, and when I woke, the police were there to rescue us."

Hailey gave her a skeptical look. "I feel like we might've missed part of the story. You guys just napped, stranded out on a yacht all alone in the dark for hours?"

Charlotte crossed her legs and focused on straightening out her tunic. "Yup." They had napped after a lot of naked time that would never be spoken of again for a variety of sexy and dark reasons.

"Are you going to see him again?" Hailey asked.

"I'm pretty busy now at work," Charlotte said, avoiding everyone's eyes. "I'm trying to build up clients for one-on-one work and he's busy too, heading back to LA soon." She forced a laugh. "It was a crazy date, but that's it. Let's hear chapter one, Hailey."

Hailey, always eager to get them started on a new book together, immediately stood with her e-reader and launched into the story. Charlotte let out a breath of relief.

After book club, they headed across the street for a drink at Garner's. It was their Thursday night tradition now. Josh was behind the bar, as usual. Now that Charlotte had spent so much time with Ty, she saw him in his older brother Josh too. Ty was a bulky inked version of Josh, though Ty had an exuberant outgoing personality, whereas Josh was the definition of low-key. Except tonight, Josh's eyes shot fire as Hailey approached the bar.

Charlotte stuck close to Hailey because the pair were always entertaining. Josh had once been a paid escort for Hailey at the many weddings she planned and, since their falling out, he'd spiked Hailey's nachos with a super-spicy pepper and "run out" of the ingredients to Hailey's favorite mojito whenever she tried to order it. Hailey was no innocent in all this, starting a rumor that he was impotent. A truce a few months ago at the New Year's Eve party had settled on Josh's part when he finally granted Hailey her favorite mojito, all ingredients accounted for.

Hailey ordered in a cheerful voice. "Hi, Josh. I'd like a mojito, please."

"All out of mojitos," Josh said in a low measured tone that spoke volumes. He was pissed, all right, in his low-key way.

Hailey stared. "What?"

He leaned close, palms on the dark cherrywood bar top, practically nose to nose with Hailey. "Every single ingredient is gone, even the mint *wilted*."

A low murmur ran through their group. Everyone knew what that meant. The women took seats near Hailey for a good view of the fireworks. They'd all been waiting for this moment since last summer. It had taken Josh a good ten months to catch on to the impotence rumor. Of course, they'd all kept it secret (girl code), and the usually flirty women that frequented the bar had been extra nice to Josh. Charlotte couldn't wait to find out who blabbed to him.

Hailey's pale blue eyes widened in a show of innocence. "But you've had all the ingredients since New Year's. Four months now." She tilted her head with a sweet smile. "I thought we took care of that little problem."

Josh's eyes narrowed into slits. "Turns out to be *bigger* than you thought."

Charlotte suppressed a laugh. Her friends fell silent.

Hailey blustered on. "I'll take a chardonnay."

Josh straightened. "All out."

"Then I'll take a pinot grigio," Hailey said gamely. When Josh didn't move, she added, "Please."

"Out of that too," he snapped.

"Sauvignon blanc?"

His lip curled. "Out, out, out."

"What can I get, then?"

He crossed his arms. "You can get a glass of water that may or may not contain my spit."

"Josh!"

He leaned close, his voice fierce enough to give a less oblivious woman chills. "I know what you did."

"Me?" Hailey squeaked.

He straightened and jabbed a finger in Hailey's direction. "And you know how I found out? Because Maggie O'Hare, that sweet seventy-something *grandmother*, took it upon herself to bring a sex therapist in here to meet with me today. And she wasn't quiet about it either!"

Everyone laughed. Oh, if only they'd been there for that! She could only imagine when Josh—

"It's not funny!" Josh snapped, shooting them a dark silencing look. It worked. His eyes landed on his sister, Mad. "And *you* knew about this all this time?"

Mad fidgeted on her bar stool. "Yeah, but I couldn't tell you. Girl code." She went to fist-bump Hailey, who shook her head, apparently still working the innocent angle. Mad turned back to Josh and added in a small voice, "It was just a joke."

Josh's focus shifted back to Hailey, and Mad visibly relaxed. "Now it all makes sense." He paced behind the bar. "I've had very few dates in the last—" he stopped and looked to the ceiling before his gaze landed back on Hailey "—since last July when I ran out of your mojito ingredients!"

Hailey kept a straight face, giving nothing away.

"And the dates I've had have been sugary sweet, which I now know is because they felt sorry for me."

Hailey tossed her hair over her shoulder. "Really, Josh, if any of those women had a lick of sense, they wouldn't believe a silly rumor—"

"That you started! Don't deny it!"

Hailey continued as if he hadn't spoken. "And would get to know you and see you're almost normal."

Josh spoke through his teeth. "You crossed the line, princess. I wondered why my tips were so high yet I was getting turned down left and right. I haven't had decent sex in months because of you."

"But you have had sex," Hailey spat.

"The gentle crappy kind," Josh snapped.

Hailey bristled, her color high. "Well! I wouldn't know anything about the crappy kind of sex. That's on you."

Josh glared again. "You'd better watch your back."

Hailey smiled her all-teeth beauty-queen smile. It popped up under high-pressure situations, a callback to her pageant training when she was a teen. "This is fixable." She turned. "Attention, ladies!" She had the full attention of their friends and a few other groups spread out around the other side of the bar. "Josh is *not*, I repeat, *not* impotent. That was just a little—" she brought her thumb and forefinger together to show how little "—joke." Unfortunately, it looked like she was saying he had a little, er, package. And then Hailey made it worse with a big exaggerated wink.

Giggling and whispering spread around the bar. Charlotte covered her mouth in a vain attempt to keep her own laughter quiet.

"Put your hand down!" Josh barked at Hailey's tiny-banana gesture. "And what's with the wink?"

"So they'd know it was a joke," Hailey said brightly. She was either completely oblivious or an evil genius. Charlotte was beginning to suspect the latter.

A muscle ticked in Josh's jaw, yet his voice was deadly calm. "No, when you say I'm not *that thing*, and then you wink, it sounds like I am."

Hailey waved that away. "No, silly. The wink means a joke. Like when you say there's no mojito ingredients with a little twinkly wink in your eye."

"There's no twinkly wink," he growled.

Hailey pushed up on the bar top and leaned over, looking around behind the bar. "I'm sure there's some mojito—"

Josh got in her face. "You owe me hot sex!"

Hailey gasped and scrambled back so fast she lost her footing. Josh moved lightning quick, reaching across the bar top and grabbing her by the upper arms. They stood like that in an almost embrace, separated by the bar, staring at each other.

Hailey's lashes fluttered down. "Thank you," she said softly.

Josh grunted and dropped his grip on her arms. "You can get a drink over at McGinty's from now on." That was a bar in Eastman, the next town over.

Hailey smiled sweetly. "I surely will." Then she gave him a big wink.

Charlotte laughed out loud. Hailey refused to leave her hometown bar. It was where she networked with a lot of people in town for her wedding planning business, whether or not a surly bartender tried to deny her sustenance.

Josh muttered some choice words.

"You're here!" a masculine voice boomed.

The hair on the back of Charlotte's neck stood up and she slowly turned to see Ty holding a black motorcycle helmet under his arm in a black leather jacket, black jeans, and black leather boots. He looked like an avenging angel.

"Can you order a chardonnay for me?" Hailey whispered to Charlotte, but she was too shocked by Ty's sudden appearance to respond. What was he doing here? He was supposed to be working in the city. Her entire body heated, every nerve tingling and on edge. *Be cool.*

Ty's gaze locked on hers from across the room. He swaggered over. "You weren't at book club. Anyway, I've got a three-day weekend. Let's go to Bermuda, soak in some sun, and drink piña coladas on the beach."

She felt woozy. Not just from the outrageous invitation and his sudden appearance. He had a black eye. She raised shaking fingers to touch his cheek. "What happened?"

"Caught a punch in a fight scene. No big. Swelling went down. You should've seen me yesterday." He looked around at all of her friends, who were watching with interest. "Hey, everybody." He turned back to her. "Well?"

She shook her head. "I'm not going to Bermuda with you."

"I will," her friends said in near unison.

Ty grinned at them. "Thanks, ladies." He turned back to her. "How about that steak dinner, then?" He was sneaky, going in with the outrageous offer only to make dinner seem an easy choice by comparison.

"Ty, no," she said quietly, not wanting to embarrass him with a public rejection. His injury, though relatively minor, was a reminder that he wasn't a good bet for a relationship. She was still considering being a mom before her window closed, and a stuntman would not be a reliable dad.

Ty turned to her friends. "Ladies, help me out here. Tell her my virtues." So much for a private conversation.

"He's shameless," Josh said.

"Reckless," Mad said.

"Okay, anything a little more positive?" Ty asked. He spotted Lauren. "C'mere, I remember you from the wedding. Lauren, right?"

Lauren nodded and crossed to his side. Ty dropped his arm over her shoulders. Lauren flushed pink and pushed her long light brown hair over her ears. "Tell her," Ty instructed.

Lauren smiled at Charlotte and said sweetly, "He enjoys happy endings."

Ty's head whipped toward Lauren. "We never...she doesn't mean—"

"And romance with the right girl," Lauren added, smiling widely. "Ty confided in me at Claire and Jake's wedding."

"Yeah, that's good," Ty said. "Keep going."

"I can't think of anything else."

Ty took his arm off Lauren's shoulders and frowned.

Hailey piped up. "He's inked and muscled." She turned to Charlotte. "You like that." She turned back to Ty. "She said she likes that."

"Ooh!" Lauren raised a finger. "I just thought of something. He can rearrange your furniture."

Ty gave Lauren a strange look. "Sure," he said slowly. "If you want me to."

"Take off your shirt and show her your muscles," Hailey urged.

Ty set his helmet on a nearby table and peeled off his jacket, tossing it over the back of a chair. He wore a dark blue T-shirt that stretched tight across his massive chest. Charlotte's mouth went dry. His gaze locked with hers as he snagged the end of the shirt.

"You take off that shirt," Josh growled, "and I'll toss you out on your ass for harassment."

Charlotte whirled. "Don't you dare!" She rushed over to Ty's side, suddenly realizing that Josh had played her. He'd never kicked anyone out and surely wouldn't kick out his own brother. Even Hailey remained at the bar, sans mojito.

Ty smiled down at her. "Hello."

"Why are you doing this?" she asked in a low voice.

"Because we connected." He tapped the end of her nose like she was cute or something. Like he had no memory of all the heavy stuff she'd confided. "And I want more of that connection. No pressure. Just some fun while I'm in town. I leave in two weeks."

She went up on tiptoe to whisper in his ear, and his arm slid around her waist, tipping her into him. Her entire body melted into his despite her determination to keep her distance. "Is this because you're hoping for second-date sex?"

His voice rumbled close. "You know how many phonies I meet? You're real. The kind of woman I respect."

She flushed at the compliment. It wasn't "you're so pretty" or "you're sexy" like most men would say. It was about respect and who she was on the inside. "I don't usually share like that," she whispered. "It was an extreme circumstance."

He released her and she shifted back to her own two feet, cooling down with the space between them. "They don't need me on set until Monday," he said. "Three-day weekend. I'll be at my dad's house in Eastman. We can just hang out." He lowered his voice, dipping his head to her ear. "Sex is off the table unless you want another hand job or a glow job. That's the female version of a blow—"

"Got it." She glanced around, hoping no one heard that.

"Because you'll glow after." He grinned.

She shook her head. "Fine, you win—"

"I always do." His brown eyes danced with playful good humor marred only by the black eye.

"Are you hurt anywhere else?" she asked.

"Just some bruises around the ribs." He gestured toward his left side.

She bit her lip, staring at his ribs covered by his shirt.

He chucked her under the chin. "Hey, if you're so worried, hang out with me for a couple of weeks and keep me out of trouble."

She caved. It was only hanging out for two weeks, not a permanent commitment. He grinned, seeming to know the moment she was on board.

She held up a hand, about to set some ground rules, when he snagged her hand and kissed the palm. A tingle ran straight up her arm at the warm touch and the slight scrape of his stubble. "We'll—" she cleared her throat "—hang out."

"Great." He squeezed her hand and then held it. "What do you do for fun on the weekend?"

She gestured around the bar to her friends. "Hang out with my friends. Here or at someone's place or sometimes we go out to dinner."

"You want me to hang out with your girl friends?"

"You don't have to—"

"I don't mind. Women love me."

"Yes, well…"

"Joking," he said with a slow nod that said he really wasn't.

"What do you do for fun?" she countered.

He looked to the ceiling. "Let's see, fun that you might like too?"

"Any kind of fun."

He met her eyes directly. "Party, long cruise on my Harley, basketball with the guys. Take your pick."

"Hmm…I'm not sure there's much overlap here."

"No backing out now. Pick one."

"We'll have dinner."

"That's it?"

"The rest to be decided."

He grabbed her wrist and lifted her arm in the air. "She said yes!" he boomed.

Her friends cheered and she blushed furiously, though she wasn't a blusher. Geez, Ty was going to take some getting used to the way he put everything out there. But she found she kind of liked his *what you see is what you get* nature. It was refreshing in a guy. He played games, yes, but mostly in good fun. He'd apologized for his one misstep and since then he'd been nothing but good to her. She was cautiously optimistic for a small bit of fun in her life before she had to make the big decisions.

10

Charlotte was a bundle of nerves on Friday night. Ty would be coming over with dinner any minute now. Even after all of the intimacy they'd shared on their first date, this second *whatever it was* had her heart hammering. There was something unexpectedly sweet about him that just got to her. She paced the house, which she'd recently cleaned, and then finally sat on the sofa, staring at the door. She smoothed nonexistent wrinkles from her pale green T-shirt. She hoped the outfit—T-shirt, black jeans, and ankle boots—said casual. Just a night hanging out at home with a gorgeous sexy man in a friendly way.

The doorbell rang and she leaped to answer it. Right on time, seven o'clock.

She took a deep calming breath and opened the door. Ty flashed a smile, his brown eyes crinkling at the corners. His black eye looked a little better. "Hey, Char," he said in a warm honey tone.

Swoon. "Hi," she breathed.

He wore an equally casual outfit—white T-shirt, faded jeans, and sneakers—and it took everything she had not to throw herself in his arms. Some part of her longed to be held by his strong arms again. His hugs swallowed her up in a good way, the best full-body embrace she'd ever felt.

"Your dinner," he said, holding up a large brown bag.

"Come in."

He stepped inside, his woodsy fresh outdoor sex scent washing over her. That cologne was powerfully erotic, or maybe that was just Ty. "Thanks for having me."

"Of course. What're we having?"

"Sushi."

"I love sushi!"

He smiled. "I knew you would."

She put a hand on her hip and asked playfully, "Why, you know everything about me?" She promptly clamped her mouth shut because he did.

He didn't seem to notice her sudden discomfort as he made himself at home on her sofa and set the dinner bag on the round glass coffee table. "What I don't know I shrewdly guess." He held up a finger. "Basic principle, we both keep fit, watch what we eat, and heavy on the protein. It was either sushi or steak, but the steak is really better freshly grilled."

He was so casual about everything she couldn't help but relax. Hanging out was no big deal. "Water okay to drink?" she asked. "I don't have any beer."

"Water is perfect. Hey, this is our second time getting together to drink a cup of water." He winked, reminding her how she'd only offered to share water when he'd first asked her out.

"Then it will be delicious," she replied and speed walked to the kitchen before he could see her blush.

A few minutes later, they dug into dinner. "What else is in the bag?" she asked. It was kind of large for just two take-out containers of sushi.

"That's the fixings for a martini, for later. Josh told me that's your favorite drink."

"Oh." Her heart kicked up, the unexpected sweetness tipping her into dangerously mushy territory. "So how's work?"

His face lit up as he spoke animatedly about the movie he was working on—a spy thriller. He was especially excited about rappelling off a skyscraper, which gave her the heebie-jeebies just thinking about it.

"How high up?" she asked.

He chewed and swallowed. "Real high. Twenty stories. It's a military-style rappel, so the goal is speed. More like jumping."

She shuddered.

"Of course, there's a harness on me and an inflatable stunt bag down below in case a rope snaps or something. It's like a big pillow."

"That's it? A pillow?" That sounded completely inadequate for a twenty-story fall. That was probably two hundred feet. She completely lost her appetite, thinking of Ty in a free fall to the city street.

She studied his profile for a moment. He was completely relaxed, at ease with the risks he took. "I don't think I could bear to watch what you do."

He glanced at her. "You see it in the movies all the time."

"I never really thought about the person actually doing that stuff."

He inclined his head. "People never do. We're the real heroes of the movie." He snagged another piece of sushi with the chopsticks and popped it in his mouth.

"I guess I always thought a lot of that stuff was just a trick of the camera. Like green screen or whatever."

After he finished chewing, he said, "Some of it is. A lot of it isn't. Depends on the movie and the budget. Obviously it's better if you can make it as realistic as possible. Like my last movie, I walked through fire."

She grabbed his arm. "No!" All his beautiful golden skin.

"Yeah. And it looks amazing on film."

"Did it hurt?"

"It's uncomfortable. We wear this protective layer under our clothes and then there's this goopy shit they slather all over us. Then whoosh! Flames. Stumble to your mark. Stop, drop, and roll. Then they spray you down with fire extinguishers."

She felt sick. "How can you do that? Do you have a death wish?"

He lifted one massive shoulder. "It's all calculated risk. My company outfit is the best. No deaths in twenty years—"

"I don't think I want to know any more." Charlotte swallowed hard, her chest tight with anxiety.

"We're all very well trained. I'm even starting to train some of the newer crew."

"Are any of the stuntmen married?"

He arched a brow. "Just one guy. Why?"

She stared at her dinner, poking at it with the chopsticks, thinking of that stuntman's wife. *How could that woman allow herself to love someone who might die? Who purposely took death-defying risks on a daily basis just for a movie? Calm down. You're not marrying Ty, you're just hanging out.*

Ty went on. "The best are the fight scenes; car-chase scenes are a close second. I love cars. Bikes too. Motorcycle bikes, not regular bikes. One time I rode a bike right up the roof of a moving car coming right at me." She sucked in a breath and he kept talking with even greater enthusiasm. "Another time I jumped off an overpass onto a moving car, no bike that time, and then ran down it."

"Ty." She closed her eyes over the terrifying images. "It's scary to think of you doing those things."

He laughed. "Glad to know you care. Don't worry. I'm quick on my feet. What scares me is the idea of a desk job. I think I'd die of boredom."

"I don't think anyone has ever died of boredom."

"Safe is way overrated." He put his chopsticks down and turned to her. "You took a chance hanging out with me again and now here we are sharing food and having a great time."

"You're really having a great time?" She'd thought staying in might be a little tame for him.

He gave her a tender smile. "Any time with you is a great time."

She blinked, a little taken aback with his easy openness. "Wow."

"What?"

"Nothing."

"I'm being sincere."

"Sorry. I'm just not used to it."

He grunted. "Better get used to it."

She didn't respond, instead finishing up her meal, her appetite returning. She wasn't used to a guy like Ty. He was getting under her skin, making her feel vulnerable yet also strangely happy. She was glad they'd decided to hang out and also glad there was a time limit with him going back to LA. She could enjoy him without getting in too deep.

They finished up dinner and Ty stood. "I'll do the dishes." He gathered the take-out containers and headed to the kitchen to toss them in the trash.

She followed behind him. "So what do you want to do now?"

"We never did get to dance together. Let's move the furniture back, put on some kickass tunes, and boogie."

Her jaw dropped. "For real?"

He dumped the trash and turned to her. "You want to go to a club instead? I know you love dancing."

She smoothed her hair. "We could do it here." She flushed. "I mean dance here."

"Then we'll do it here." His lips curled into a sexy knowing smile.

She couldn't help but smile. The delicious butterfly feeling was back—lust, excitement, and anxiety all rolled together.

And then he started rearranging her furniture, working those powerful muscles.

She watched with some amusement. "Lauren said you would be handy at rearranging the furniture."

He flashed a wide smile. "I'm handy for a lot of things."

"I bet."

His eyes locked with hers. "I think you know."

Heat pooled between her legs. Yeah, she knew. "I thought we were just hanging out today," she croaked.

"Sure are," he said easily.

"Then why do you keep reminding me about—"

"Your long-awaited orgasm?"

"I was going to say what happened on the boat." She waved a hand in the air. "Can we not talk about this?"

He lifted the coffee table and set it by the sofa against the wall. "You brought it up."

"No, you implied you were handy with a ton of innuendo."

He finished pushing all her furniture out of the way and rolled up the area rug. "I am handy." He gestured to his handiwork. "Now we have a dance floor. Nice hardwood, by the way. Put on your favorite music and let's see your moves."

She felt suddenly shy. It was so weird to be shy about dancing, but she usually danced at a place where dance was expected—a wedding or a club—not at home with one man who knew too much watching her.

"Preferably something from this century," he added, kicking off his sneakers. He ran and skidded across the hardwood floor in his socks.

"What are you saying I'm old school?"

"If the granny glasses fit." He did a few arm windmills. "I saw your playlist."

"Just because a song is old doesn't mean it's not good anymore," she grumbled, heading over to her speaker dock and pressing the button on her iPod for her workout playlist —a lot of hard, pumping club jams.

Ty started bobbing his head in time to the music. "Bump and grind, baby."

"I don't bump and grind. I dance."

He wiggled his fingers for her to join him, dancing a bit in place with a sexy come-hither look. She felt frozen for some reason. Like somehow dancing meant more than dancing. The man was weaving some kind of spell over her.

The lights flickered on and off. Oh, shit. Not the power. She did *not* want to be stuck a second time in the dark with Ty. It wasn't raining, but sometimes wind could take the power out.

"You look terrified," Ty said with a laugh. "What do you think's going to happen if we're in the dark? You already told me all your secrets."

"You said it was in the vault."

"It is. It's just us." He crossed to her and took her hand. Then he turned the music up loud, brought her to the center of the room, and turned off the overhead lights, so it was just the soft light from the end table. He took her hand and twirled her around slowly, completely off from the fast beat of the music thrumming through the room. Her heart raced. She needed to get this excess anxious energy out.

"We're moving too slow," she said.

He moved right up into her space, dancing faster now, smiling down at her, not seeming to find her past or her current complicated life unsettling at all. In fact, when he looked at her like that, she felt light and carefree.

She lifted her arms over her head and danced.

"Go, Char, go, Char." He egged her on in his playful way and she really let loose, enjoying herself. Surprisingly he kept up with her, even lifting her up in a big swooping move. Damn, they really could go on *Dancing with the Stars*. She giggled, thinking of the headlines—*Living room boogie pair makes it big!*

She lost herself to dancing. Song after song as she and Ty figured out how to move together, sometimes laughing at an awkward bump and sometimes smoldering at a sudden intensity in the way their bodies moved.

Her playlist ended after an hour and the ensuing silence was startling. Her ears took a moment to adjust. She pushed the sweaty hair out of her eyes and smiled at him. "That was quite a workout."

He grinned. "You're a better dancer than me, but it was fun."

She bumped him with her hip. "You kept up pretty well. Not many men can dance at all."

He hauled her up against his side and kissed her temple. "Ready for a drink?"

"Yeah, I'll get us some water."

"Cool. I'll get the martini." He pulled up his shirt and wiped the sweat off his face. His abs looked so lickable. Her gaze caught on a couple of bruises on his left side and she quickly turned away.

She grabbed two glasses of water, returning to the living room, and stopped to watch the amazing Ty Moves Furniture show. She admired the rippling muscles of his shoulders, biceps, even his forearms as he put all her furniture back in place. See, he was okay, she reassured herself. His bruises didn't seem to bother him in the slightest.

"Thank you," she said.

"No problem." He finished, sat on the sofa, and dug into the bag.

"Here, take a drink." She handed him the glass.

He chugged it down, handing it back to her a few moments later. "Thanks."

"You're welcome," she murmured, taking a long swallow of her own drink.

He mixed the ingredients in a martini shaker, shook it up, and poured two drinks. He'd even brought two plastic martini glasses.

"You think of everything," she said.

"Wait," he said, retrieving a small container of toothpicks and another small container of green olives. "Now I have everything." He set the olives in place in the glasses. "Bottoms up."

She took a glass and sipped. "It's good."

He sipped his drink and made a face. "This is what you like?"

She couldn't help but laugh. "You did a good job."

He stuck his tongue out and set the glass down. "I'll bring beer next time."

"Sounds fair." She sipped her drink, happy and relaxed. Her endorphins must really be kicking in from all that dancing.

Time flew by as they talked easily. Ty told her about his house out in LA and how much he loved his work, even though he missed hanging with his brothers and honorary brothers, the guys he grew up with. It was hard for her to understand as an only child. But for him his brothers were like a part of him and, after a while, he needed to get in a visit or he actually felt out of sorts. He especially missed his mouthy twerp of a sister, he confided.

"Don't tell Mad," Ty said in a conspiratorial tone, "but she's my favorite. Strong and fierce. Ya gotta respect a fourth-degree blackbelt."

She smiled, warmed by the sweet confession. "You surely do." She thought back to the way Ty teased Mad, but he also hugged her enthusiastically and ruffled her hair. He looked out for her in his big-brother way, she already knew that.

Eventually it got late and she couldn't hold back a yawn. She'd worked today, leading a few Zumba classes and working with her private clients. Not to mention their dancing in the living room.

"You're tired," Ty said. "I'll go."

"You can stay if you want," she blurted. She wasn't quite ready to say goodbye.

He gazed at her for a long moment, seemed to come to a decision, and packed up the martini stuff. "This was great." He stood. "Thanks for having me."

"You're going? For real?"

"For real. I told ya, no pressure, just hanging out. You want to come to my basketball game with the guys tomorrow?"

"You mean to watch you play?"

He tucked the bag under his arm. "You can watch, or you can play. I'll make sure no one plows you down."

"I'll just watch." She wasn't great at basketball and the idea of playing with a bunch of sweaty aggressive guys didn't really appeal.

"Great. I'll pick you up at noon. Game's at the park not far from here."

"Okay." She stood and walked with him to the front door. "Thanks for dinner and everything."

He dipped his head, kissed her cheek, and rumbled in her ear, "My pleasure."

She got a hot shiver, grabbed a hold of his upper arms, closed her eyes, and tilted her head up for a kiss—

Nothing.

She opened her eyes. He gave her a quick smile and then he left.

She couldn't quite believe it. No hot goodbye kiss?

No groping when they were dancing either.

This was weird.

Seriously weird. After the boat and her orgasm and her being all naked and him only in a towel. It was almost gentlemanly. Omigod, he was a gentleman! His upbringing had kicked in. But why now and not before? Was he *not* into her now that he knew so much, or was it the opposite, he was *so* into her that he wanted to treat her extra special?

She sighed and crossed her arms, hugging herself. She couldn't remember ever feeling so good yet so unsatisfied. Maybe that was his game. Making her desire him so much that she made the first move. *Well played, Ty.* If that was his game, it worked. She couldn't wait to see him again and she definitely couldn't wait to touch him again skin on skin. And with that thought came the immediate decision to wait on the sperm-donor single-mom route. Clearly she longed for some fun in her life and it would be good to have that before she made a decision on having a baby. A month or two delay wouldn't hurt. Then, with a clear head and no regrets, she'd make a plan for her future.

She headed to the bathroom, got out the birth control pills she'd been waffling over for the past couple of months, and took one.

11

———

Charlotte was ridiculously happy that Ty showed up exactly on time the next day. It made him seem reliable, a rare commodity nowadays, especially with the men she normally dated. He wore a black tee and black basketball shorts with high-top red basketball shoes.

"Ready?" he asked from her front porch.

"Ready." She went up on tiptoe and kissed his scruffy cheek.

He flashed a smile. "What was that for?"

"Just happy to see you, I guess."

"Missing me so soon, eh? It was a pretty kickass date." He turned and strutted down the front sidewalk.

"I thought we were just hanging out," she said, locking the front door.

"That's what I said."

She smiled to herself, turned, and stopped short when she saw the Harley in her driveway.

"Ever ride?" he asked.

"No. Where's your car?"

"The Mustang was Park's on loan just for the day. I keep my old Harley here to get around when I'm in town. Didn't you notice it yesterday?"

She shook her head. She'd been too wound up about their hanging-out/kickass date to notice.

"It's a short easy ride," he said. "Believe me, I'm in full control. I push them to the limits in stunts."

Her heart fluttered, worried all over again about his beautiful body splattered on pavement. She suddenly felt light-headed.

Ty slid an arm around her waist. "You okay? You look pale."

She took a deep breath. "Every time you tell me what you do for a living, I feel a little dizzy."

He kissed her temple. "Aww, you worry about me. Ain't you sweet?"

No one had ever called her sweet. "I'm not trying to be sweet."

"You just naturally are. Ready to ride?"

She broke out in a sweat. "Are you going to do anything risky?"

He framed her face with both hands and gazed into her eyes. "With you, never."

She felt breathless at the intensity of his gaze, but she believed him. "Okay."

She followed him to the bike. He put on her helmet for her and checked to make sure it was fastened properly.

"Adorable," he pronounced.

He threw one leg over the bike, sat down, and hitched a thumb for her to do the same. "Use the foot pegs and keep your feet there."

"Got it." She got on behind him, immediately hugging his waist. The solid warmth of his broad back calmed her nerves. The seat was wide and comfortable for two.

"Don't lean against the turn," he said over his shoulder. "Just relax and follow my lead."

"Okay."

He gunned the motor and made an easy turn out of her driveway. It was a beautiful sunny spring day and the light breeze felt full of promise. Within minutes, Charlotte was surprised to find herself completely relaxed. Between Ty's heat and the vibrations between her legs, it was a *very* good ride.

Only ten minutes or so later, he pulled into the long driveway of the park. A few more turns and he parked. She stepped off the bike and he followed, taking off his helmet and turning to her. "How was it for you?" he asked in a sultry voice.

"It was amazing," she returned in a seductive purr.

He grinned and gestured for her helmet. After he secured them to the bike, he entwined his fingers with hers and headed toward the basketball court. "I'm pretty sure you met everyone at Claire and Jake's wedding, but just in case, here's a quick recap." He pointed to the court, where three guys were already practicing free throws. "That's Marcus; he's always here first, even though he has to travel furthest. He lives in lower Manhattan. That's how much he loves us. There's Logan; you know Josh. Not here yet, but later you'll see Park, Mad, Alex, and Ethan."

"That's cool that Mad can keep up with you guys," she said. "I mean, since she's so petite." Mad was only five foot four.

"Are you kidding? She's one of the best players out there. What she lacks in height she makes up for in speed and sneaky steals. Besides, she's been playing since she could hold a ball."

"Is that everyone you call brother?"

"Jake, of course." That was Josh's identical twin. He was with his wife, Claire, at her latest movie location. "Did you hear he's getting into the business now with Claire's production company?" Claire Jordan was a major movie star and sometime book club member. Jake had been helping out with the marketing for Claire's company.

"You mean he's going to produce a movie?" she asked.

"Thinking about it. He's also toying with the idea of pitching some TV shows."

"That's really cool!"

"Yeah, we'll see. Depends on what he comes up with." He stopped by the side of the court, watching the guys. "Ben had to work. Zach used to play too, but he's out of touch out in no man's land."

"You mean jail?" she whispered.

Ty's head swiveled toward her.

"Ty!" Josh called, raising a hand in greeting. "Hey, Charlotte, you playing?"

"No, I'm just watching. Thanks for the martini. Ty told me that was your suggestion."

Josh dribbled a ball back and forth between his legs. "Had to give him an advantage the way you were shooting him down cold."

"Did you ever think there might be a reason for that?" she asked.

Josh straightened and held the ball under one arm. "Never crossed my mind."

"She's way into me now," Ty boasted loud enough for the entire park to hear. Before she could counter that maybe it was the other way around, he was gone, giving Josh a big pound-on-the-back bro hug.

Ty stole the ball from Josh, took three huge steps toward the basket, and *swish*!

"Impressive," she said.

Ty pointed to her. "That was for you, baby."

Charlotte flushed. "Thank you?"

"Show-off," Josh said.

"I'll just sit over here," she said, pointing to the bleachers. Yeah, she was definitely not joining in when the guys could play that well. She'd just annoy them. She hadn't even attempted the game since high school gym.

One by one, the guys arrived, dropping off bottled waters or thermoses on the bleachers. They were surprisingly choreographed as they warmed up, like maybe they were running drills they all knew. She figured they must be waiting for someone before the game started. She tried to remember each guy again. The Campbells had a strong family resemblance to each other with dark brown hair, dark brown eyes, and muscular athletic builds. Only Logan had light brown hair. Oh, Alex was missing. He was a single dad to a two-year-old. That could definitely make a guy late.

Ty stopped by the bleachers and snagged someone else's bottled water. She knew he hadn't brought one. He took a long swallow. "How're you doing? Not too bored?"

"I'm fine."

"Sure you don't want to play? Always more fun to join in the action than sit on the sidelines."

"I'm okay."

"If Alex doesn't show soon, we might need you to even up the teams. Don't worry, I'll cover you."

She had no idea how he'd cover her—most guys played aggressively, eager to win—and fervently hoped Alex showed. At least she was wearing jeans and sneakers, though she didn't want to sweat through her pretty embroidered button-down shirt.

Ty turned. "Hey, you finally made it!"

Alex was pushing a stroller with his daughter, Vivian, in it. As they got closer, Charlotte realized Vivian was asleep. "Sorry I'm late. The nanny quit."

"Again?" Ty asked.

"I know," Alex said wearily. "Anyway, I just stopped by to watch for a bit and then I'll head out. I don't want to leave her by herself."

"I'll watch her," Charlotte said. "It's no problem. I'm just sitting here anyway."

"You would?" Alex said, his expression going from weary to hopeful. "Thank you. If she wakes, just tell her Daddy's right over here playing ball."

"You think she remembers me from the wedding?" Charlotte asked. It had been almost four months ago.

"I'm not sure," Alex said. "That's why you point me out first thing. She'll be pissed if she doesn't see me right away."

"Okay."

He dug around in the back of the stroller. "Here's her sippy cup and some Cheerios."

"Got it."

"Viv will be fine," Ty said, slinging an arm over Alex's shoulders. "Char loves kids."

She jolted at the casual remark. They headed off to the court.

It wasn't like Ty had ever seen her with kids. She'd only babysat for preschoolers back in high school. A baby was a distant fantasy. Who knew if she'd be any good at it? She glanced over at Vivian sleeping peacefully with a small square light blue blanket, fraying at the edges, tucked against her cheek. Another yellow fleece blanket covered the rest of her. Her cheeks were pink, her lips parted slightly, and her light brown hair was longer than the last time Charlotte had seen her. Now there were just waves in her hair, the baby curls already growing out. Charlotte's heart squeezed. Vivian looked like an angel.

A few minutes later, Park and Mad arrived. Charlotte gave them a quick hello. Neither one of them seemed surprised to see her. Finally everyone was there and the game began. But Charlotte barely saw it. Instead she kept a careful eye on Vivian in case she woke up.

The moment she did, Charlotte leaned down to her and whispered, "Your daddy's right there playing ball." She pointed.

The little girl scrunched up her face like she was going to cry.

"See?" She quickly turned the stroller so she could see better. "There he is playing ball with your uncles and aunt."

Vivian slowly sat up and looked around.

"You want your sippy cup and snack?"

Vivian nodded. She gave them to her. The little girl sipped, dropped the cup in her stroller, and easily lifted the plastic lid off the container. Charlotte relaxed. This wouldn't be so hard. Five minutes later the Cheerios were gone and Vivian handed back her empties. Easy enough. What an independent little girl.

Then she tried to climb out of the stroller.

"Wait! I'll help you." Charlotte pulled back the blankets and saw there was a little seat belt. She undid it and lifted her out. Vivian's hand tangled in Charlotte's hair, tugging it a little, but she didn't mind.

"Swing," Vivian said.

Charlotte looked around and spotted a playground in the distance. "Let me ask your daddy."

"Swing!"

"Let's just check in with Daddy."

"SWING!"

The girl had some lungs. And a dogged persistence Charlotte suspected was a Campbell gene. She stopped by the edge of the court with Vivian in her arms and waved to Alex.

"Time-out," Alex said and jogged over, sweat pouring off him. "Hey, pumpkin." He kissed Vivian's cheek. "You remember Charlotte? She's Aunt Mad's friend. And Uncle Ty's too." He winked at Charlotte.

Vivian could care less. "Swing."

"Is it okay to take her?" Charlotte asked.

"If you don't mind," Alex said. "Don't turn your back for a minute, though; she's fast and fearless."

"Got it."

"You don't have to carry her." He ruffled Vivian's hair. "You're a big girl now, right, Viv? My superstrong girl." He held up a fist for a fist bump.

Vivian fist bumped. "Strong girl."

Charlotte smiled, loving the sentiment. Teach 'em young to be kickass. No wonder Mad was such a confident strong woman. She was probably raised that way, the only girl in a houseful of older brothers and her dad.

Alex gestured to Charlotte to put Viv down.

Charlotte set her on the ground and the girl took off, running full speed toward the playground. Damn, she was fast for someone with such little legs. She took off after her.

Ty took a short water break after the first half of the game and caught sight of Charlotte playing with Viv on the playground. His niece was shrieking with delight as Charlotte chased her in circles around the slide and then suddenly turned, looking surprised to see her behind her. Viv cracked up, bending over with her laughter. He watched as they went a few rounds like that, entranced at the beautiful sight. Charlotte was a natural.

"Earth to Ty!" Park hollered from the court.

Ty shook his head, raised a hand to the guys, and headed back to the game.

His younger brother by two years, Logan, elbowed him. "See, this is why you never bring a woman to your game. Now you suck."

Ty elbowed him back. "I do not suck. Prepare to lose."

Alex and Logan tipped off at center and they played the second half, but he couldn't keep his mind on the game. His gaze kept pulling back to Charlotte and Viv having a grand old time together. His team lost and the guys all blamed him. He didn't even care, which wasn't like him.

"Next time," he said, wiping the sweat from his face with the bottom of his shirt. He stepped off the court. Charlotte and Viv headed straight toward him, holding hands, both of them smiling.

That is the woman I'm going to marry.

The thought shocked the hell out of him. He quickly averted his eyes. *Whoa. Hit the brakes.*

Alex appeared at his side. A moment later, Charlotte and Viv stood in front of them, still holding hands, seeming happy they found each other. The sight of the woman longing for a child and his motherless niece happy together made Ty's chest ache. He focused on Alex instead.

Alex scooped up Viv. "You have fun?" She nodded and he turned to Charlotte for confirmation.

Charlotte smiled. "We had a great time. She's super sneaky. She kept surprising me." Viv reached for Charlotte and Alex handed her over. Viv gave Charlotte a tight squeeze around her neck.

Viv pulled back and patted Charlotte's cheek. "Come over?"

"Not this time," Alex said. "We've got stuff to do."

"Next time," Charlotte said.

Viv grabbed Charlotte's long hair with both hands, lifting locks of it and watching them fall. Charlotte's hair was pretty, long and silky. Viv probably wasn't used to seeing long hair with only Mad's hair to mess with, which barely reached her shoulders. Viv never knew her mom. Tammy had died during the C-section having her.

Charlotte extricated Viv's fingers from her hair and handed her back to Alex.

"So long," Alex said. "Thanks again, Charlotte."

"No problem." Charlotte smiled, watching them go. Finally her gaze returned to him. "Did you have fun?"

He couldn't speak for a moment, his chest aching with the enormity of all he felt. This couldn't be love so soon. They'd only known each other for a couple of weeks. Love had only happened for him once before and he'd gotten burned. His ex had been using him to get a meeting with a director, stringing Ty along for two months, playing the long game for a career opportunity. What he felt for his ex, even in the beginning, was insignificant compared to the way he felt right now about Charlotte.

If he had any sense of self-preservation, he'd drop her off and never look back.

"You okay?" Charlotte asked.

This was crazy. "Yeah," he mumbled.

She inspected his black eye and eyed his ribs on his left side covered by his shirt, seeming to remember everywhere he'd been injured.

"Sure?" she asked softly.

Hope, a dangerous thing, filled his heart.

"I'm sure." He kissed her, unable to resist before he belatedly remembered he was drenched in sweat. "I should head home and shower. You want to meet up for dinner tonight?"

Clearly he had no sense of self-preservation.

"What about this afternoon?" she asked, and he fell a little harder. She wanted to spend all her time with him. There were no brakes on this thing. "I thought we were hanging out this weekend."

He couldn't help but smile. Big time. "You want more of me so soon?"

"You're only in town for two more weeks, so I figure we shouldn't waste time."

He kissed the end of her nose. "You're damn sweet."

She shook her head, trying to deny it. He wasn't buying it, but he didn't argue the point. Instead he said his goodbyes and headed to his bike, eager to get back to hanging out with Charlotte just the two of them.

"You were a natural with Viv," he said, entwining his fingers with hers. "She was having a blast."

She got serious. "I had a good time."

He wasn't the most intuitive guy, but given what Char had told him before, he knew she was worried about having kids. "Ya know, my dad mentored a lot of kids and they truly felt like family. It doesn't have to be your blood to feel real."

She grimaced. "This is quite possibly my least favorite topic in the world. Can we not talk about it?"

"You got it. So the plan is, I stop home, shower, and change clothes then back to your place for whatever you want."

"You want to cook dinner together? I could teach you a simple roast chicken recipe."

"Absolutely."

"You would've agreed to anything, wouldn't you?"

"Yup."

They got to his bike and he handed her the helmet. She put it on, looking pleased to be going for a ride. See? Already he was a good influence, opening her up to new experiences. What woman could resist a motorcycle-riding, orgasm-giving man?

He made the short drive to his dad's place, let himself in, and left Charlotte to relax on the sofa. Upstairs, he stopped short outside of the bathroom. His dad was in the shower. He was on a reverse schedule, working night shift as part-time security guard, sleeping until afternoon, and then showering. Ty threw some clothes in a duffel bag and headed back downstairs.

"Shower's taken," he said. "Okay if I take one at your place?"

"Of course."

Once they got to Charlotte's place, she settled on the sofa with an e-reader. He hoped she was reading one of those smutty books they liked in her book club. Then she'd be all hot for him. *Stop that shit.* Yes, he wanted her, badly, but he didn't want to be all about the physical with Charlotte. As crazy and fast as it was, he knew this was the woman for him with a certainty he'd never had with any of his relationships. His only regret was screwing things up the first time he'd met her at Claire and Jake's wedding. They'd lost time because of his own stupid fault. From now on he was going to do every-thing right. A slow getting to know each other. A strong foun-dation of friendship. The rest would fall into place when the time was right. Not because of his own usual slick moves. They'd have to work out the long-distance thing, but it wasn't insurmountable with regular visits, phone calls, texts and all that.

He turned on the shower and gave it a few moments to warm up. The bathroom was decorated kinda girly, every-thing matching—towels, soap dispenser, toothbrush holder, even the small trash can—white with light red flowers on a tree branch. Maybe cherry blossoms but less pink. He didn't know, but it felt cozy. His own house in LA was all black and white with steel accents.

The shower started to steam. He quickly stripped, slid back the glass door, and stepped inside. He soaked his hair and grabbed the shampoo. Pomegranate? He sniffed it. Great, now he was going to smell all fruity and girly. He should've brought some of his own shampoo.

"I think I'm gonna smell like you," he hollered.

A moment later, the door popped open. "What's that?"

"I'm gonna smell fruity like you." He closed his eyes, lath-ered, and rinsed the shampoo out of his hair, so he wouldn't be tempted to coax her in with him. When he opened his eyes, Charlotte stood a few feet away, staring at him through the glass, in her bare feet. Holy crap, she was unbuttoning her shirt. He went instantly hard. Who the hell was he kidding with this slow getting-to-know-you stuff? He should've known it would come to this. The attraction was too intense to ignore.

Again he was condom-less. Idiot! He should've tossed some in his duffel bag. Maybe she had a box around here. No, they should wait. With someone special like Charlotte, it shouldn't be all about the physical. That was for quick flings, not for the serious stuff.

"Don't come any closer," he ordered.

She stepped closer.

He swallowed. He could *not* resist that kind of temptation.

But he was determined to get to know her and not just fuck her brains out. He should get an award for this kind of restraint. He slid the shower door aside just enough to poke his head out. "Baby, wait for me out there."

She licked her lips. "You are *hung*."

"Course I am, everything's in proportion. Go wait for me out there."

She peeled her shirt off, dropping it on the floor. Just a white lace bra that barely contained her full beautiful breasts. Her nipples tightened under his gaze, pointing right at him.

He forced his gaze back to her eyes. "I can see you're getting horny. I'll give you a hand job as soon as I'm done here. Promise." She slid the bra straps off her shoulders, and he felt desperate. "Baby, please. I'll give you a glow job, just—"

The bra sprang open and she peeled it off, her gaze raking all over him.

"Put that back on," he demanded.

She set it with her shirt on a hook on the back of the door. He admired the curvy lines of her back flaring out to her hips in tight jeans.

She turned back to him and undid the button on the jeans.

He took a deep breath, making one last attempt at the slow getting-to-know-you thing. "Sex is off the table. We're just hanging out. Remember?" His voice cracked at the end there, just like his control was going to crack if she didn't stop.

She slid her hands through her hair, shaking it out, and then ran her hands down her neck, over her breasts, cupping them together and lifting them. His cock pulsed. Her hands slid down her stomach and on to the waistband of her jeans. If those jeans dropped, it was over.

"I don't have protection," he said urgently. "Do you have a condom?"

She shook her head and unzipped the jeans.

"Just give me a few minutes and I'll help you out. Wait for me in your bedroom. Okay? After I'm dressed."

She wiggled the jeans down her hips. A scrap of white lace panties. His fingers tingled with the need to touch.

"I went back on the pill," she said. *Bye-bye, panties.* They hit the floor next to her jeans. Game fucking over.

"Get in here, woman. You do that for me?"

She shrugged and crossed to him. "I just decided I didn't want to be a single mom right now."

He smiled widely. "Because you're into me."

"Maybe."

She stepped into the shower and he pulled her in for a hug, feeling all warm and gooey that she was imagining a different kind of future because of him.

She kissed along his neck. "You're awfully sweet."

He ran his hands up and down her back, loving feeling her all pressed against him. He shifted them so she'd get some of the warm water too. "Who said that? I'll break their neck."

"I said it."

"Oh, then you're mistaken." He kissed her and bit down on her lower lip. She made a sexy little noise. Then he kissed her for real, deep and hot, sliding his fingers into her long silky hair.

She broke the kiss and smiled against his mouth. "I can't wait to feel you inside me."

And then there were no words. Only a hot blur of sensation as he took what she offered. She was aggressive, kissing him roughly, her hands everywhere. He slid his hand between her legs, testing her readiness. Damn, she was so wet for him. She moaned in his mouth, practically climbing his body. He lifted her, pressing her back against the wall, and took her in one swift thrust. They both moaned as they finally joined together. Her head tipped back, her eyes closed. He kissed along her throat, pressing deep within her.

"Yes," she moaned. "More."

"You feel so good. I want to make it last." He kept an easy pace, wanting to give her maximum pleasure. He eased back just enough to slip a hand between them, stroking her. She made sexy needy noises that made him even thicker and harder, her gaze unfocused. He watched as she surrendered to pleasure, much faster than the first time he'd been with her, her jaw slack, her eyes dilating and then fluttering closed. He loved that. He was damn proud of it, knowing it was her trust in him that made her let go. And then she went off with a sharp cry and he took what he needed, driving deep over and over. He cupped her face with one hand and she opened her eyes, her breath ragged like his. Her eyes went soft, gazing back at him. The rush of pleasure and emotion hit like a damn tidal wave. He gripped her by the hips, pumping with an explosive release, and then sank against her, buried deep.

When he lifted his head, he swore they were surrounded by an almost divine aura—everything was glowing, their bodies, the steamy air around them, even the white tile.

She hugged him with her arms and legs, giving him a squeeze, before resting her head on his shoulder.

He never wanted to let her go.

12

Charlotte's leg jiggled restlessly, even surrounded by her friends for their Thursday night post-book club drinks at Garner's. How could she relax knowing Ty was rappelling down a skyscraper tonight? Everything felt off; even her martini tasted bitter. She pushed her drink away. She'd gotten in too deep, let herself feel too much. Now she lived in a torturous state of anxiety every time he went to work, until she knew he was safe again. She forced her mind back to her precious happy memories with Ty.

Their first weekend together at her place, they'd made dinner together and made love multiple times. She got a hot flash just thinking about it. His goal was *always* to maximize her pleasure. He actually said that in his bold way of putting everything out there. After that, she completely relaxed, letting him do as he pleased. He let her do as she pleased and they moved together as easily as a dance. When would she ever get to experience that rare synchronicity again?

Outside of the bedroom, she'd thought he'd be more domineering with his loud voice and ballsy attitude, used to doing things his way, but he was nearly the opposite—laid-back and accommodating. He even offered to watch whatever movie was her favorite. She put on *Gone with the Wind* just to test his sincerity and he actually got into it. Any man who'd sit through a chick flick and actually let himself get into it was a keeper as far as she was concerned. Last weekend they'd stayed at his hotel in the city and he'd taken her shopping because that was her favorite thing to do in Manhattan. A man who shopped!

She rested her head on her hand, her eyes unfocused as a swoony sigh escaped. He was so affectionate and attentive. Gorgeous and sexy. She honestly didn't think men like him existed.

And she'd almost missed out on all of that. If they hadn't gotten stranded on the boat, bringing an intimacy in the dark that she rarely allowed in any of her relationships, if he hadn't made such an effort to hang out with her again, she never would've known. She would've just kept right on thinking he was an arrogant guy who played games like the first time they'd met. It made her appreciate what they had even more.

It had been a very long time since she'd let herself feel so much for a man, but somehow Ty had gotten under her defenses and into her heart. If he didn't survive this stunt, he might never know how much she felt for him. Her hands formed fists, her nails digging into her palms. *Don't think that way. You'll jinx him.*

Maybe he already knew how she felt. He had this way of holding her head, his fingers spanning from temple to jaw as he gazed into her eyes, making it impossible to hide all she was feeling. He held her like that often, when he was about to kiss her, when they were making love, after one of his enthusiastic bear hugs. And she felt that love coming back to her too, like it was building on both of their parts. Even though Ty talked about the future like they'd still be together, casually mentioning places he wanted to take her in LA or stuff they could do together in the summer, which was months away, she still felt the deadline for him returning to LA was hanging over both of their heads every moment they were together. And now it was almost here.

Mad elbowed her. "You okay?"

Charlotte turned. "I'm fine. Just worried about Ty. He's doing a twenty-story fast climb down a skyscraper tonight."

"Don't worry. They've got wires on him and all that safety shit."

"I can't help it," Charlotte replied in a tight voice. "I feel sick every time he tells me about one of his stunts."

"You really like him, huh?" Mad asked.

Charlotte nodded, the lump in her throat making it difficult to speak.

Mad bumped her shoulder, just as physical as Ty. "You let me know if he does something dumbass like break your heart. I'll kick his butt."

A reluctant smile tugged at her lips. "Thanks, Mad."

"Ooh," Mad chortled, "watch this. Hailey brought a peace offering for Josh."

Charlotte exchanged a smile with Mad, welcoming the distraction. "She must really love her mojitos." They giggled. Now the rumor around town was that all that impotence talk was just a cover for the real problem—his tiny banana. Hailey had done nothing to encourage the "tiny" rumor, swearing on her life that it wasn't true, though she always hastened to add, "Not that I have any personal experience." Josh had been less than pleased with this result, but was at a loss as to how to prove his manhood to the many women who frequented the bar short of whipping it out. His only consolation was giving Hailey the cold shoulder and denying all her drink requests.

Hailey set a large clear plastic container on the bar top in front of Josh. Inside were chocolate chip cookies. Everyone in the book club knew how delicious they were.

Josh gave her a squinty-eyed glare.

Hailey smiled in return. "I've brought you a gift to make up for our tiny spat."

"It's *not* tiny," Josh said through his teeth.

The women tittered.

"I know you're a foodie," Hailey went on despite the pink creeping up her neck. She took the lid off and held out the container. "Try one. If you like it, I'll email you the recipe with the secret ingredient."

Josh eyed her suspiciously. "You eat one first, princess."

Hailey pasted on a smile. "But it's your gift." She waved the container around under his nose. "It's for you."

"They're delicious," Mad put in. The women all agreed heartily.

"Then let's see you eat one," Josh challenged Mad.

Mad hesitated. "But they're for you."

"Josh, they're not poison!" Hailey exclaimed. "I'm trying to make amends because of our little issue."

"It's not little, I assure you," Josh growled.

Bright pink dotted Hailey's cheeks, matching her neck. "Please accept this in the spirit it's given. The proportion of brown sugar to white sugar makes them nice and soft. They just melt in your mouth. If you like them, I'm happy to email you the recipe."

Josh was not having it. "You first."

Charlotte watched—it seemed the entire bar had quieted to watch—as Hailey took the tiniest of bites and chewed. Hailey nodded her approval of the deliciousness. "Mmm."

"Eat the whole thing," Josh ordered.

"Can I get a drink of water?" Hailey asked.

"Swallow first," Josh said.

"I really need a drink of water," Hailey insisted, hand on her throat.

Josh's gaze dipped under the bar as he reached for a glass. Hailey took that opportunity to spit the cookie into a napkin.

Josh jerked upright, filling the glass while taking all of them in. "Did she swallow?"

"That's what he said," Mad quipped.

"Yes," Charlotte assured him. Everyone chimed in their agreement. Girl code.

Josh slid Hailey her glass of water and she beamed. "Thank you." She took a drink, set her glass down, and pushed the container closer to Josh. "Go ahead. I'm sure you'll enjoy them."

"After you eat a whole cookie in front of me," Josh said.

Hailey tossed her hair over her shoulder. "Of all the ungrateful—"

"I'll have one," Trav O'Hare, a handsome guy maybe forty, said from down the far end of the bar. Trav was well known locally, a landscape architect married to the daughter of the owner of Garner's. Charlotte knew Hailey would be extra careful with such a well-connected member of the community.

"Me too," the dark-haired gorgeous guy next to him said.

"Rico's wife banned sugar at his house," Trav said. "He's desperate."

Josh shot Hailey a sly look. "There you go, princess. Share the wealth."

"See?" Hailey said haughtily. "Not everyone's suspicious like you."

Josh gestured for her to go ahead.

Hailey turned to Trav and Rico. "These were made special for Josh. It's his present."

Trav and Rico exchanged a grin.

Josh leaned his palms on the bar top and got in Hailey's face. "You're going to have to try a *lot* harder to outsmart me. I'm onto you."

Hailey gulped audibly.

Josh straightened and went on. "Your sweet do-gooder persona is a cover-up for a devious strategist. Well, guess what, princess? So am I."

Hailey rallied quickly. "That's you, Josh, not me. I'm acting out of pure intentions!"

"Purely devious intentions," Josh countered.

Hailey lifted her chin. "Geez. Try to make amends and this is the thanks I get."

Josh shoved the container back in Hailey's hands. "Email me the recipe minus whatever poison you tossed in there."

Hailey's jaw dropped. "Poison! I would never—"

"Bugs, spit, beans, laxative, what?"

The bar went silent, all of them eager to hear what she'd done.

Hailey looked around at all the curious eyes and back to

Josh's accusing eyes. "It's raisins, okay? I substituted raisins for the chocolate chips and it tastes wrong and disgusting!"

Josh barked out a laugh. "Maybe you're not as devious as I thought."

Hailey harrumphed, seeming annoyed she'd had to admit the raisin thing without even getting the pleasure of watching Josh's disgusted face when he tried one.

Josh grabbed a rag and cleaned off the bar top. "Still not getting a mojito out of me."

Hailey huffed. "Then I guess we're back to square one."

Josh stilled and met her eyes. "Oh no, we're up a whole 'nother level. Watch your pretty behind, princess."

She lifted her chin. "That's impossible. It's way back there." She hitched a thumb over her shoulder.

Josh cracked a smile. "I'll watch it for you."

"You always do," Hailey replied. She stood, leaving the cookies, and gestured to all of them. "Come on, ladies, back to my house for the good stuff, fudge brownies."

Charlotte inclined her head for everyone to follow. Give the girl her dramatic exit. Besides, the entertaining part of the evening was over.

Hailey sashayed out the door.

Charlotte glanced back to see Josh followed through watching Hailey's behind as promised.

Ty was flying high all week at work. Both because he was crazy in love with Charlotte and because he was literally flying in a harness, practicing rappelling down a skyscraper from a few stories up while the director and cinematographer worked out how they wanted the shot to look. It was all preparation for the ultimate twenty-story rappelling scene. Now it was Thursday night, the second-to-last day for him on location. He'd be leaving tomorrow night. Charlotte would meet him for dinner before his red-eye flight and then that was it for a while. He hoped she could get some time off to visit him because he had another gig right after this for at least six weeks in LA.

"All right, Ty, we're ready when you are," the director called. "Check in with Gary and then head on up for the scene." It was a night scene, the trickiest to film, but the director wanted the lights of the city. A scaffold nearby lit up the shot.

"You got it." He rappelled down to the ground and unhooked the safety wire from the front of his harness. Then he spoke to Gary, the stunt coordinator, reviewing the entire scene from the moment he dropped from the window, pretending to lose his grip on the rope and dangling one-handed before grasping the rope with both hands and rappelling down quickly and stealthily. If things went south, which they rarely did, there was a huge inflatable stunt bag under him.

He headed into the building, chatting with the A-list actor he was doubling for, and they rode the elevator up together. The guy loved stunts and wished he could do more, but the studio didn't want to risk damage to their star.

Once he got the all clear from the twentieth floor, he peered out the window and looked down. His adrenaline spiked at the risk he was about to face down and conquer. It was the biggest rush. He wished Charlotte was here to see him, but she cringed every time he mentioned work. She had to get used to it sooner or later. He was young enough to have years ahead of him in the business. His boss hadn't stepped back from stunts until he turned fifty.

One last safety check. The climbing rope tested and tugged. His safety wire—the same one he'd rehearsed with—reattached and tested. He flexed his fingers in their protective gloves and did his usual pumped-up ritual, taking a few deep breaths and then jumping up and down in place. He signaled he was ready, got the return signal it was a go and rushed forward, quickly scaling the window, turning, and then let himself fall, one hand on the rope, the other flailing as planned. Something snapped. The safety wire flew past his face. And then he was swinging one-handed, out of control.

He scrambled to get both hands on the rope, desperate to control the descent, still hoping to save the shot. He finally got it, snagging the rope two-handed, his body swinging in toward the building. His feet hit hard at an odd angle against the glass and pain shot up like fire from his left ankle. He bounced away and then swung back, body slamming into the building, the breath knocked out of him. His grip on the rope loosened, dropping, dropping, the momentum too much. He grappled for a better grip in a near panic. Shit. He glanced down and saw the inflatable stunt bag was close enough. Gary was hollering to just get down. Controlled landing was always better than a panicky one. His training kicked in. He let go of the rope—seconds of free fall, the wind whistling past his ears—and then *whoomp!* Softish landing, his body enveloped by the inflatable bag.

He lay perfectly still, his heart galloping madly. He tested out his left ankle and hissed out a breath at the pain. Dammit all to hell. The crew gathered to help him out of the bag.

"Wait," he said. "Left ankle might be broken."

"We got you, Ty," Gary said.

They got him out of the bag and upright. Ty winced when he tried to put weight on it and Gary helped him over to a chair to wait for the ambulance. He was suddenly glad Charlotte hadn't been there to witness it. He'd wait until tomorrow to tell her when he felt less shitty. She was already damn touchy about his job.

13

—————

Ty waited to call Charlotte until just before she left Clover Park to meet him for dinner in the city on what was supposed to be his last day in town. Turned out to be a severe ankle sprain, not broken, which was great, but he still couldn't work his LA gig. Too much climbing and big jumps for his current condition. She'd texted him last night, saying only, "Thinking of you." He'd replied, "You too. Wiped out. Goodnight."

Now he had to break it gently to her. As soon as she answered the phone, he said, "Good news."

"What's that?" she asked with a note of caution.

"Looks like I'll be in town a bit longer, so we don't have to say goodbye yet."

"What's wrong?"

"I've got some time off."

"Ty! Are you in the hospital?"

"Relax. I'm at the hotel."

"Oh, for a minute there I thought something bad happened. Why do you suddenly have time off? Did your other job fall through?"

"Nothing serious. Just an ankle sprain."

Dead silence.

"You still there?"

"Yes." He heard her take a shaky breath. "What happened?"

"One of the ropes snapped when I was rappelling down the building, so I slammed into the building at a bad angle. Anyway since I can't work my LA gig, I'm staying an extra week. I still have to go back to LA. My boss wants me to train some of the newer stunt people. So come on over. I'm just sitting around waiting for your sexy self."

"Okay. I just need a little time to catch my breath."

"You working out?"

"No! I'm trying not to hyperventilate thinking about you rappelling down a building when the rope snapped. How high up were you?"

"I don't know. It's a bit of a blur. Maybe eighteen stories up."

She sucked in air.

"But I grappled with the main rope for a while, so I didn't actually drop into the pillow until much later. I'm okay. Promise. Come see for yourself."

"I will," she muttered. "Bye."

That wasn't too bad, he thought. Maybe she would get used to everything that came with his job. He ordered up some room service once he figured she was close. This would all be fine. They'd hang out a little more and he figured they could still have fun in bed.

Only when he opened the hotel door, Charlotte took one look at his crutches and ankle brace and her lower lip wobbled.

He rushed to reassure her. "Don't cry, baby. I'm fine. Honest. The crutches are just for forty-eight hours. Only twenty-four more hours now."

She glared at him through shiny eyes. He shifted on his crutches so she could come in, unsure if she was going to cry or go off on him.

Her voice was low and controlled. "I can't do this, Ty."

His gut clenched. "Can't do what?"

"I can't worry about you all the time risking life and limb just for a movie."

"It's my job."

She dashed at her eye with a fist. "And I can't handle getting a phone call that you're in the hospital or dead."

"C'mere, let's talk." He made his way over to the bed, set his crutches to the side, and sat down. He patted the spot next to him.

She joined him, folding her hands in her lap and staring at them glumly. "I'm sorry. I can't pretend to be happy that you're staying longer for this reason."

"You don't have to freak out. It could've been much worse."

"I know! You could be dead or paralyzed. Geez, Ty, I'm trying to be understanding, but I can't bear it. I feel nauseous every time you go to work."

Her hands were gripped so tightly together they were turning white. He pried them apart and took her hand in his. "Baby, I've broken tons of stuff." He pointed out all his past healed injuries. "My ribs, my wrist, my other leg. That's what they pay me the big bucks for so the talent doesn't have to. The doc says I'll be good as new in four to six weeks."

She took a sniffly breath like she was trying not to cry.

"Some good came out of it. We've got another week together now."

She nodded, staring at the floor.

"And then I have to go back to LA, but you can visit as soon as you get time off. You can stay at my house. I'll get the plane tickets. Just say the word."

She looked to the ceiling and wiped under her eyes.

He feared she was about to lose it and the last thing he wanted was to be the cause of her tears. "We're going to have a future together."

She pressed her lips tightly together.

There was a knock at the door.

"That's room service," he said, reaching for his crutches.

She stood. "I'll get it."

She brought everything in and set it up at the small round

table with two chairs. They ate their healthy skinless chicken and vegetables in silence. See, they even liked the same foods, he thought but didn't say. She seemed too upset for light conversation.

When they finished dinner, he reached across the table and took both her hands in his, giving them a gentle squeeze. "You're not going to bail on me just because you're worried, are you?"

"I'm afraid you're going to bail on me."

"Never."

"Not on purpose. I mean if something happened to you."

He slowly shook his head. "Nothing's going to happen to me. And we're going to make this work. Now just think about this, don't answer right away, but what if you moved to LA with me and worked as a personal trainer out there? I know a ton of people in the industry that would love to work with you."

"Why don't *you* work as a personal trainer for them?" Her voice rose in enthusiasm. "They know you. You used to be a personal trainer."

"Because I'm a stuntman! That's who I am! You're trying to change me."

She pulled her hands from his. "I can't be with someone who risks their life every day just for a movie."

"So I'm supposed to give up who I am so you'll feel better?"

"Your job is not you, Ty. I want you to be you in a safer way."

None of this sat well with him. Being a stuntman was who he was; he lived and breathed the job. He narrowed his eyes. "You can make it sound as pretty as you want, but what it comes down to is you want me to give up my dream job just because you're a worrier."

"I want you in my life. Our future—"

"You mean *your* version of our future! Why're you being like this? I thought you were different, but you're just like every other woman trying to mold her man—"

"Do *not* lump me in with your other women. I'm saying

this—" She stopped herself, took a deep breath, and when she met his eyes, he felt a cool distance. "Let's not fight. We only have a week. Who knows what will happen after that?"

He frowned. It sounded like she didn't think it would work out long term, but he let it go for now. He didn't want to argue the same thing over and over. He was definitely *not* giving up a career he loved. He didn't want to give up Charlotte either, but how could he be with someone who didn't support his dream?

After a week of living with Ty at her place, Charlotte knew without a doubt that she loved him and found herself on the verge of tears way too many times at the idea of losing him. Not because he didn't want to be with her, because he was taken from her. Who knew what his job would bring him next? Whatever some damn movie director dreamed up, Ty would put himself at risk to do it. She wished she could let it go, but it was impossible.

Their last night together was bittersweet. She felt like crying just getting ready for bed, even though Ty was in her bedroom right this very minute. Maybe because she knew she had to let him go. Logic told her that for at least the next six weeks or so, he'd be safe because of his ankle sprain, but it didn't stop the intense anxiety she had for his safety.

She stepped into her bedroom, where Ty was lying shirtless in all his glorious muscular inked splendor. She turned off the light and slid under the covers. He tucked her into his full-body embrace, side by side, his arms and one leg wrapping around her. He was completely naked, his heat radiating through her T-shirt and cotton sleep pants.

"I'm going to miss you, Char. I wish you could get time off sooner."

She gave him a little squeeze. "Me too." She didn't have vacation time until July. It was better that way. It would give her the space she needed to try to get over him. But right now, all tucked tight against him, all she felt was overwhelming love.

He stroked her hair and cupped the side of her face. "If I can manage it, I'll fly home in two weeks."

"You still call Connecticut home when you've lived in LA all this time?"

"You're my home now."

Her eyes welled.

"It's true," Ty said against her lips and then kissed her. He was king of the distracting kiss. She let him, eager to escape her dark thoughts. She was addicted to what he made her feel, only wanting more the more she was with him. And in a surprising twist, he was extremely attuned to her emotions, becoming more tender with her when she needed it.

He got her naked, still kissing everywhere he could reach and then cupping her breasts with both hands. She closed her eyes, sinking into the pure pleasure of his touch as he massaged and stroked. He shifted down, taking her breast into his mouth, suckling deep. Mindless pleasure pushed her worries away. He was here now, real and solid and doing delicious things to her body. He did the same to her other breast while his hands ran down her sides, her hips, and then cupped her firmly between the legs. His fingers stroked her expertly, knowing exactly what she liked, and she shuddered, sparks of sensation radiating out from her core. In no time at all, he had her teetering on the edge. She tensed, knowing a monster peak was close, not knowing if he'd give it to her. He pulled away.

Her eyes flew open. He loved to bring her to orgasm, but he also loved to bring her close and pull her back, playing with her until she was practically hollering at him to give it to her. It was how he maximized her pleasure. It was also how he made her crazy.

"Don't toy with me," she said. "Not tonight."

He smiled lazily and sat up. "Why not tonight?"

Because this might be our last night together.

She kept the thought to herself, instead climbing into his lap and wrapping her legs around him. He held her by the hips, lifting her and then guiding her down onto him. Their eyes locked and they both moaned at the intense connection as she took him in fully. He gave her a moment before angling her hips for his first thrust, stroking her G-spot. She cried out, her nails digging into his back, still shocked at how quickly he zeroed in on all of her hot spots. He kept going, his large hands gripping her hips, over and over and over. White-hot pleasure. Brain meltdown. She whimpered incoherently, on fire, lost in all-consuming pleasure.

"Charlotte, baby, look at me."

She met his dark eyes, her heart kicking hard at the love she saw there, though he'd never said the words. He didn't have to, it was clear as day.

His voice was rough and gravelly. "Yeah, you know it, deep down." He cupped her face from temple to jaw, his other hand gripping her hip. Another deep stroking that had her gasping. "You feel that, right?"

"Y-yes."

"What do you feel?"

He thrust again. She was so close. She couldn't speak, her breath coming in small pants now. *No more toying*, she thought.

"You feel the love," he prompted.

She nodded and then cried out as he gave her another deep stroking.

"Should I tell you my secret?" He held her firmly, one hand on her head, one hand on her hip, rocking her in a slow rhythm, and she was going under, too much, the pressure building in her core, her body owned by him.

His voice was low and deep, the only thing tethering her before the explosion. "Here's my secret..." She trembled uncontrollably as he rocked into her. "Hold on one more minute, I've got you. I'm going to tell you my secret and then I'm going to let you come."

He stilled and she let out a cry of protest.

"Don't be mad, baby. Before me you didn't even get the big O. Now I give it to you multiple times a night."

She glared at him.

He kissed her and thrust again. She gasped, back on the knife edge of release. He broke the kiss. "Here's my secret. You listening?"

"Yes, yes, yes," she chanted, rocking on her own.

He clamped a hand on her hip, stilling her. "I've loved you since the night you shared all your deep secrets with me. I want to marry you, kids, dog, the whole deal. That's how much I love you."

Her jaw dropped as she stared at him in utter shock.

"And now you get your orgasm," he said.

She didn't even know what he did. One moment she was staring blankly, the next a full-body shudder ripped through her as she came hard and long, Ty guiding her through wave after wave of pleasure. And then he let out a hoarse cry, exploding inside her, holding her tight.

A few moments later, he lifted her up, giving her space to untangle her legs from around him and then lay back, taking her with him, stretched out fully on top of his delicious heat. His arms wrapped around her and she sighed, resting her head on his chest and listening to the solid thump of his heart.

He spoke, his voice rumbling in his chest. "Did I scare you away?"

"I can't move."

"Good. I planned it that way. I'm in no condition to chase you running for the hills."

She laughed.

He stroked her hair. "We have a good future ahead of us."

No man had ever spoken so powerfully straight from the heart. She closed her stinging eyes, wishing she could believe in the sentiment.

Charlotte tried to keep it together after Ty went back to LA. She really did. She went to work. She hung out with her friends. She even worked out extra, trying to get some endorphins going, but all she got was tired and weepy. She hated feeling like this, so emotional, so devastated with his absence after they'd only been together for a month. Oh, but what a month. She tried to hide her sadness when he called each night, but he knew her well. The very first time her voice wobbled, three days in, he told her it was definite that he'd be flying back home in two weeks.

"Put it on your calendar," he said. "You can count on it. I'm booking the flight now. Let's see. I can be there by Saturday afternoon. Time change is working in my favor."

"I don't need to put it on my calendar. I'll be counting down the days."

"Aren't you sweet?"

"You're the sweet one flying back here just because I'm being overly emotional."

"I'm not doing it for you. I haven't had a good orgasm in three days. You understand I have to self-serve without my favorite rider."

She laughed. Somehow he could always make her laugh.

Now the day was finally here, a beautiful early May day with the sun shining and the birds singing and everything was glorious. She was nearly giddy with happiness. He'd arranged a car service from the airport to her house, so there was nothing to do but wait. She headed out for a run, needing to let out some of her excess energy. She made her way to Main street in Clover Park. She liked to look through the downtown shop windows and veer off into Baldwin Park. She thought about the month she'd had with Ty, the boat date, his crazy offer to take her to Bermuda that turned into a weekend of hanging out and sex, lots and lots of sex. And love too. She loved him so damn much. And he loved her so much he wanted to marry her. She held that truth close to her heart, giving her the courage she needed to share everything with him. She had so much to catch him up on, so much planning they needed to do for their future, but mostly she just wanted to be back in his arms.

After her run, she showered, cleaned the house top to bottom, showered again, and finally it was time. She opened the door on that sunny afternoon to the love of her life, arms open, smiling from ear to ear.

Her smile dropped. She slapped a hand over her mouth, her stomach rolling. Ty was on crutches with a cast on his right leg.

14

———

Ty took one look at Charlotte's wide eyes, her hand covering her mouth in horror, and knew he'd done the right thing not telling her about his mishap over the phone. Now he could comfort her in person.

"Don't freak out," he said. "It's just a fibula break. I'll be in a walking boot in two weeks. It's not even a full leg cast. See? Just below the knee."

She dropped her hand. "Ty! What happened? Why didn't you tell me? We talk every night."

"Can I come in?"

She stepped back and he swung his large wheeled suitcase in ahead of him before he swung in on the crutches. He turned to her, and she bit her lower lip, her eyes fixed on his cast.

"The good news is I have the next six weeks off," he said. "And my left ankle is almost good as new." He pointed to the leg without the cast in an effort to remind her he was a quick healer. The sprained ankle was nothing compared to the pain of bone cracking.

She blinked rapidly, her eyes shiny. "What happened?"

"Motorcycle jump went south. I was demonstrating for the new guy. Maybe I was a little ambitious with the jump."

"Were you in the hospital?" she asked in a small voice.

"Yeah, emergency room. Just in and out. It's really not a big deal."

"It *is* a big deal! I can't believe you didn't tell me."

"Let's sit down and talk," he said, making his way to the sofa. He wanted to hold her and explain everything and he couldn't do that on his feet. He set his crutches to the side and took a seat.

She joined him and stared straight ahead. "I don't understand why you wouldn't mention any of this."

He slid an arm around her shoulders. "I know how you worry about me. I wanted to wait and tell you in person so you could see for yourself I'm fine." He pulled her close and kissed her temple. "Plus I wanted to hold you in case you got upset."

She straightened and dashed at her eyes with a fist. "Well, I am upset."

"I know." He wrapped his arms around her, pulling her close for a hug. "I'm sorry I didn't tell you when it happened."

"When did it happen?"

"Tuesday."

She pulled away. "So we talked and texted for four days and you just pretended everything was fine?"

"Everything was fine." Her eyes flashed and he rushed to explain. "Okay, it wasn't totally fine. I felt shitty and I didn't want you to worry. I would've been here sooner, but the doc wanted me to wait a few days before flying. Something to do with the plaster cast and swelling."

"Ty, we need to be honest with each other. You said you were what you see is what you get and I liked that about you."

"Okay, okay, next time I'll call you from the emergency room."

Her face crumpled.

"I didn't mean that bad," he said, stroking her hair. "I thought you wanted to know right away. Anyway, look at the bright side. Now we get six weeks together."

She looked off in the distance, her hands gripped tightly together in her lap.

He felt her withdrawing, pulling into her defensive shell, and he wanted feisty, happy, in-love-with-him Charlotte back. Not that she ever said she loved him, but he was pretty sure she did. Otherwise why would she care so much what happened to him?

"Relax," he said. "It could've been much worse."

Her head swiveled toward him. "Why do you always say that? Is that supposed to make me feel better?"

"Nothing's going to happen to me," he said. "Nothing serious anyway."

Dead silence. She looked off in the distance again.

"Char, please, look at me. Say something."

She swallowed and a tear leaked out. He lifted his hand to wipe her tear away, but she pulled back, brushing it away like it was an annoyance.

"Char—"

"I love you."

His heart was in his throat. It was the first time she'd said it back to him, but he feared there was bad news heading his way because she didn't sound happy about it.

"I love you too," he said cautiously.

She spoke earnestly. "I want you to be around in the future, for our future. I want you to think about a lower risk job *for us*. I just found you and I don't want to lose you." Her voice choked. "You're too important to lose."

He frowned. "You knew who I was when you met me. Just don't think about what I do."

"I can't stop thinking about it!" She jabbed a finger in his direction. "And don't try to tell me you're perfectly safe. In the six weeks we've been together, you've gotten a black eye, a sprained ankle, and a broken leg. You're never perfectly safe."

"That was just bad luck. Usually I'm just bumped and bruised. Regular icing and I'm good as new."

She gave him a skeptical look. "You showed me all your healed injuries."

"Yeah, I got those over the course of *ten years*. That's not bad at all. I'm good at my job."

"And how long do you think you'll be so lucky? With just broken bones and bruises?"

"My boss worked stunts until he was fifty."

"Why fifty?"

"He broke his back." She gasped, and he rushed on. "That's him, not me. Baby, you're going to have to get used to me getting bruised a bit. It comes with the territory."

"A broken back is not 'bruised a bit!'" She gestured wildly. "Don't ask me to get used to it! I tried! I can't!"

He raised a brow. "Don't you think you're overreacting?"

She leapt off the sofa and stalked out of the room toward her bedroom.

"Dammit, Charlotte, where the hell are you going?" He let out a breath of exasperation. "I can't chase you around on crutches and I'm too tired to break down a door!" he hollered after her.

She disappeared from view. He leaned back on the sofa and rolled his head to the side. "Just finish the conversation!" he barked.

He knew this was a deal breaker and he wanted her on his side. He didn't want to lose her or his job. He just had to explain it better, persuade her to his way of thinking.

She returned, striding toward him, her dark eyes locked on his with a seriously kickass expression. His heart kicked up, simultaneously turned on and worried she was about to give him the axe.

She stopped in front of him. "You know how you said you want to marry me, kids, dog, the whole deal?"

His heart warmed. She was going to say it back. *Finally.* "Yes."

"I want the same thing."

He smiled. "Great."

She whipped her hand from behind her back, holding a plastic white stick up to him with two bright pink lines. "I'm pregnant."

15

———

"No."

"Yes," Charlotte assured him. "I just found out this morning." She stared at the test and beamed at how bright the two pink lines were. "It's a miracle."

Ty grabbed her and hauled her into his lap, tucking her legs to the side. "But you said you were on the pill."

She set the beautiful test on the coffee table and turned back to him. "I was, but I started it when we started, and it turns out sometimes it can still happen in the beginning. I mean, when you first go back on the pill." She bit her lip, anxiously waiting for his reaction. It had taken her a little time to comprehend what happened. She'd skipped her period, which had happened before, but something told her just to check with a test to be sure. While she'd waited for the test results, a quick online search told her it was possible to get pregnant if you'd just started taking the pill. She'd been off it for a few months because of the surgery and her waffling over in vitro.

Ty was eerily silent, staring straight ahead in an expression of utter shock. Maybe she should've eased him into the conversation, but she wanted him to understand why he was so important for her and their baby's future. She wasn't trying to change him. She just wanted him to be alive and well for their future.

"Ty?"

He slowly shook his head. "I thought you couldn't get pregnant."

"There was only a very small chance. One percent. It's a miracle!" She smiled tightly, still a little worried that he wasn't as happy as she was.

Suddenly he crushed her to him, pinning her tight, one hand cupping her head to his chest, the other arm wrapped around her torso. She smiled to herself, glad he was over the shock.

"Holy crap," he said. "This is…amazing!"

She tried to lift her head, and he loosened his hold. "You're happy?" she asked.

"Damn right I'm happy. Are you kidding? I've always wanted kids. Look at my huge-ass family and now I get my own. Our family." He smiled, looking bemused. "Ha! I'm the one percent. *Boom*. It's all those good orgasms I rocked through your body. It gave my swimmers lots of good vibrations."

She laughed. "I'm so happy. I just…I still can't believe it."

He hugged her again, and she snuggled in, her head on his shoulder.

"I gave you what you most wanted," he said with a note of pride.

"You did." She found herself beaming again. "The best present ever."

"When do you think it happened?"

"I don't know. We had a lot of sex."

"I bet it was that first time in the shower. There was this glow over everything."

She giggled. He was so romantic.

"There was!" He tilted her head up for a kiss. "Come back with me to LA."

"I want to stay here. My doctor is here, my friends—"

"I'm in LA," he snapped.

She took a deep breath, about to explain herself when he went on in a much gentler tone.

"You're going to need to scale back at work anyway with the pregnancy and after. Let me take care of you. I want us to be a team."

"Yes. Absolutely. I want to be a team. Okay, let me explain—"

"We're getting married right away. Get Hailey to plan something super cool super quick. Wait. Let me do it right. Shoot. I can't go down on one knee in a cast. And I don't have a ring. Just pretend, okay?" He framed her face with both hands and gazed into her eyes. "Will you marry me?"

"Yes," she said right away.

He flashed a smile before his mouth claimed hers, hot and urgent. His hands started to roam. When he lifted the back of her shirt from the waistband of her jeans, she reached back to stop him. She needed to talk to him first.

His mouth trailed to her ear, kissing along the way before taking her earlobe in his teeth. "Take this stuff off, baby," he whispered. "I can't wait to be with you."

"We need to talk."

"Later." He wrapped his hand in her hair and tilted her head back, exposing her throat to his kisses. Desire spiked within her even as her brain screamed at her to make sure he understood her situation.

"Ty, this is important." He loosened his grip on her hair and she met his heated gaze. "Can you listen, please?"

He stroked her bottom lip with his thumb and then kissed it. "What?"

The words tumbled out in a rush. "The doctor warned me if I ever did get pregnant, I'd be considered high risk because of the endometriosis. I'd really like to stay here with my doctor and the hospital in the city. It's the best for neonatal care. Plus my friends are here. In LA I'd just be waiting for you to come home and worried about you too."

His grip on her tightened. "What kind of high risk?"

Charlotte rubbed his arm. "I don't want you to worry. Chances are—"

"Tell me!"

She chose her words carefully, knowing his brother Alex had lost Tammy during the C-section. "Early labor is the one I'm most worried about. That's why the neonatal care is important. That's what they call newborn care for premature babies."

"So we could…lose the baby?"

"Chances are good—"

"What else?" he asked through his teeth.

She took a deep breath. "I could get high blood pressure, bleeding, and maybe need a C-section."

"No, no, NO," he said as if the force of his words could stop all of it from happening.

"The doctor will keep a close eye on me. I might need bed rest later on. I'd like to be home where I have my friends. They're the family I chose."

"Nothing's going to happen to you. Not on my watch." He wrapped her in a hug for long moments before pulling back and stroking her face, her neck, and down her arms. It wasn't sexual, more like he needed reassurance that she was okay. He slid his hands to her shoulders and down her back.

"Char," he croaked, his expression pained, "I had no idea you could be in danger. I feel like this is my fault."

"It was a happy accident," she said. "Nobody's fault."

His eyes watered. "I can't bear it if…"

She stroked his stubbled jaw. "No. We're going to think positive." She pressed her lips together for a moment, again choosing her words carefully. She didn't want him freaking out because of what had happened to Tammy. "I knew the risks. I accept them. I'm otherwise in good health and my chances are good for a healthy pregnancy. I'm going to see the doctor on Monday. You're welcome to come with me and ask any questions you might have."

He cupped her jaw, his voice hoarse. "I don't want you to be high risk."

She put her hand on top of his, holding it there. "Me either. It's just the way it is."

He blinked a few times, his eyes watering with unshed

tears. "Now I know how you felt when you said you didn't like my high-risk job."

"Sucks, doesn't it?"

He blew out a breath. "Yeah, it does."

"You see why I need you safe." She put a hand on her stomach. "For both of us."

He rested his forehead against hers. "We need a plan for all contingencies."

"What do you mean?"

"I'll take care of everything." He slid her off his lap and onto the sofa.

"We should make a plan together."

He snagged his crutches. "Don't move," he ordered. "You're going to stay off your feet as much as possible."

"Ty, don't be silly. I feel fine. I took a run this morning."

His gaze cut to hers. "Nope. I want you to sit still for the next nine months so you don't shake anything up in there."

"Are you serious?"

He jabbed a crutch in her direction. "Stay."

She rolled her eyes. "You're being ridiculous."

"I'm taking over cooking and cleaning."

She covered her delight with a quick frown. "I don't know—"

"I know," he said in a voice that brooked no argument. "Relax. That's your job now."

She put her feet up on the coffee table. "If you insist."

His jaw was set with determination. So sexy. "I do."

"Thank you."

He stared for a moment like he wasn't sure if she'd really conceded the point before crossing back to her and giving her a quick kiss. "Thank *you* for the best gift ever."

She had a feeling they'd be thanking each other for this gift for a long time.

~

Charlotte was enjoying a cooking show when the doorbell rang a short while after her big talk with Ty. She opened it to find her friends gathered on the front porch. "Hi," she said, surprised to see them. They'd already hung out last night at the movies and the night before at book club.

Hailey spoke first. "Ty texted me with the message, and I quote, emergency smut club meeting at Charlotte's house." She pursed her lips. "Does he know we're called the Happy Endings Book Club? Please explain we're classy ladies."

"Yeah," Mad said. "We could've been called SLUTS." That was her idea for the book club, Super Lovers of Underrated Terrific Stories.

Hailey whirled. "Would you stop reminding everyone of that awful name?" She turned back to Charlotte. "May we come in?"

Charlotte stepped back. "Of course." She'd been planning on telling her friends her big news, but she'd wanted Ty to be the first to know. She was just bursting with the news, though, and very happy to share. The moment she knew she was pregnant, something in her shifted, a cause greater than herself, that made her want to open up to her friends. Sure, they'd had a lot of good times together, but Charlotte had always held part of herself back, her natural protective reserve after her fucked-up past. Now it was all about the future.

Ty appeared in the living room from the kitchen. "Hello, ladies." He crossed to Charlotte. "Let's get you back to the sofa." He inclined his head.

"What happened to you?" Mad barked at Ty.

Ty tucked his crutches under one arm and answered even as he gave Charlotte a nudge toward the sofa with one hand. "Motorcycle jump gone bad," Ty replied. "Six weeks and I'm all good."

"How big a jump?" Mad asked.

"Obviously too big," Ty said. He made his way over to where Charlotte now sat in the center of the sofa. "You okay? Can I get you anything?"

She smiled. "I'm okay, thanks."

He nodded once. "I'll be in the bedroom, making some calls." He maneuvered out of the way so her friends could join her. Hailey sat on one side of her, Mad on the other, and everyone else—Lauren, Carrie, Ally, Missy, Sabrina, and Lexi —sat cross-legged around her coffee table.

Lauren's eyes bugged out, spotting the pregnancy test. "Omigod! Are you pregnant?"

Charlotte laughed and exchanged a happy smile with Ty before turning to her friends. "Yes."

"Make sure they're part of the plan," Ty said before heading down the hall toward her bedroom.

The women erupted in conversation, talking over each other as they showered her with congratulations quickly followed by questions. She held up a hand. "Please, one at a time."

Hailey piped up right away. "Did he propose? Please let me plan your wedding."

Mad leaned around Charlotte to shoot Hailey a dark look. "She means congratulations." She stared at Charlotte. "Wow, I can't believe Ty's going to be a dad."

"Yes, congratulations!" Hailey hugged her. "I knew there was something there. Two physical people, both of you enjoy working out and a healthy lifestyle. I predicted this match!" She lifted a finger. "In fact, I think I might've helped it along by speaking so highly of Ty. Am I right?"

Charlotte gave her that one. "Sure."

"We're so happy for you," Lauren said, wrapping her long light brown hair around her hand. "Is Ty happy too?"

Charlotte nodded, smiling like a fool. "He is." She glanced down the hallway, where Ty had disappeared, probably to make plans for their future. She turned back to her friends. "You guys, he is so sweet and tender. I've never met a man like him."

"Wait, my brother Ty?" Mad asked. "The one who told Park he'd kick his ass if he touched me? That guy?"

"He was only looking out for you," Charlotte said. "He loves Park like a brother, you know that. He just wanted Park to step up and he did."

Mad tsked. "I could have done without the interference."

"So that's why we're here?" Hailey asked. "This is all

happy news. I must confess I was a little worried about the emergency nature of this meeting."

Charlotte got serious.

Hailey grabbed her arm. "Should I be worried?"

Charlotte took a deep breath. "I want to be real with you. I find it hard to open up to people, but I need to, starting now."

Hailey's eyes widened. "What is it? Are you feeling okay?"

"I'm great!" Charlotte flashed a smile. "Okay, let me start at the beginning. Back in February when I missed our book club meeting, it was because I was recovering from surgery."

"Surgery!" Hailey exclaimed.

"Why didn't you tell us? We could've helped you!" Lauren exclaimed.

"Because I'm not used to leaning on anyone," Charlotte said. "It was laparoscopic, which makes it less invasive. Anyway, it was because of severe endometriosis. Very painful periods. They took out a lot of scar tissue and cysts. Later the doctor told me it would be difficult for me to become pregnant. Like only a one percent chance. She recommended I think about in vitro sooner rather than later. I'm a little older than you all, thirty-one."

"That's not that old," Lauren said in a soothing voice. The women all murmured agreement.

Charlotte inclined her head. "Thanks. For fertility, age makes a big difference. I was considering doing in vitro with a sperm donor before I missed my window, and then I met Ty." She found herself smiling again. "And he was just... amazing. I can't even believe how much I love him. Even before he knew about the pregnancy—by the way, we both just found out today—he told me he wanted a future with me, marriage, kids, dog, the whole deal."

The women exclaimed excitedly over this news. "Sisters!" Mad exclaimed, high-fiving Charlotte.

"Are you engaged?" Hailey asked, squirming with excitement.

"Yes, and we want you to plan it as soon as possible," Charlotte said.

Hailey squealed and whipped out her phone. "I'll set up an appointment for both of you right now."

"Can you wait on that?" Charlotte asked. "I need to share a little more."

Hailey's head shot up, her jubilant expression fading. "What is it? Are you okay?"

Charlotte stared at the bright pink lines on the pregnancy test. So much hope and promise in two little lines. She lifted her head. "I'm thrilled about the pregnancy, but here's the part I need you all for. I already know I'm high risk. I want to stay here with my doctor, and the hospital in the city is the best for high-risk pregnancies. As much as I want to be with Ty, I don't want to move out to LA while I'm pregnant. I could get put on bed rest and I don't know anyone there."

"You know Ty," Mad said. "He'll help for sure."

"Yes, but he'll also be working," Charlotte said. "And this is just one of those times when I need to be…" She couldn't speak for a moment with all the emotion clogging her throat. "I've never asked for help from anyone before, but I'm asking now, hoping you'll all be there to help me get through whatever this pregnancy brings."

The women all rushed to assure her they'd see her through the whole thing.

"Huddle up," Mad said, standing and bringing them all in for a group hug. Mad put her hand in the center of the circle. "Hands in, bitches got your back on three." She counted off.

"Bitches got your back!" the women chorused.

Charlotte's eyes welled, tears leaking out. That must be why she'd been so emotional the last couple of weeks. Hormones. It wasn't just Ty heading back to LA. She found herself blurting everything she usually kept buried deep. "You ladies are like the sisters I never had. I love you all so much."

The tears must've been contagious. Soon everyone was crying and taking turns hugging and congratulating her. Finally they all settled back in their seats. Her friends kept smiling at her, as happy as she was, it seemed.

Hailey put a hand on her arm. "Are you scared?"

"I'm a little scared," Charlotte admitted, "but mostly crazy happy."

Carrie, a young blonde woman with glasses, piped up. "Don't forget I'm a pediatric nurse. I can stay overnight whenever I'm not working. Whatever you need, Char."

"Thank you," Charlotte said, near tears again.

"Knock wood it doesn't happen—" Lauren knocked wood on the coffee table even though it was glass "—but if you end up on bed rest, I'll organize us in shifts to visit and bring you food."

"Thank you, everyone," Charlotte said. Somehow knowing she had a little human to look out for made it easier to open up about what she needed. "The thing that scares me most of all is Ty's job. It's so dangerous. I want him around for this."

"It's just a broken leg," Mad said. "That's happened before."

"People die from stunts gone wrong," Charlotte said.

"You want him to give up his job when he's got a kid on the way?" Mad asked. "That doesn't sound like a good idea."

"Not completely," Charlotte said. "I want him to do something safer. Like be a personal trainer. He can't do his job forever."

Mad shook her head. "He used to be a personal trainer. He got bored. You don't want him to feel restless and bored forced into a job he hates, do you?"

Charlotte thought about that. Both she and Ty were high risk now. She was willing to accept risk for herself for the reward of the baby at the end. He loved being a stuntman and was willing to take that risk for a job he loved. They were the same that way. Shit. She got it now. She was asking him to love her and accept her high-risk situation, so that meant she had to do the same for him. She had to allow herself to love him unconditionally, accepting that he might die doing what he loved. She wasn't happy about it, but there it was. She didn't want to be the reason he gave up his dream career and definitely didn't want him to resent her and the baby.

She suddenly realized everyone was looking at her expectantly. "Of course I want Ty to be happy. I just worry with both of us being high risk. We'll work it out."

"Is there a chance you might…die?" Mad whispered.

"I don't know," Charlotte said. "Maybe. I guess there's more of a chance. I didn't talk to the doctor yet."

"How can you not know?" Mad barked.

Charlotte turned to Mad, shocked at her friend's tone. "Pregnancy and birth are always risky."

"No, you said *you* were high risk," Mad snapped. "What does that mean?"

Charlotte spoke carefully, not wanting to alarm Mad given what had happened to Tammy. "The risks I know about so far are manageable. The baby could be born premature. I might need a C-section. I could get preeclampsia, that's high blood pressure. I could hemorrhage."

Mad hissed out a breath.

Charlotte rushed on. "But with good care and a good support system, I should be fine. And I'm sure I have both."

"C-section," Mad said in a hushed voice. "That's how Tammy died, having Viv."

Lauren gasped. "Viv never knew her mom? Poor thing." The women murmured their sympathies for Alex and Viv.

"Ty must be freaking out," Mad said. "Oh, Charlotte." Her voice choked and she swore a blue streak, dashing tears from her eyes with her fists.

Her friends all stared at Charlotte for a long solemn moment.

"But the odds are still good for a healthy pregnancy," Charlotte assured them. "I just need to be monitored closely." She hadn't known Tammy and she was much too excited over her little miracle to spend time dwelling on the risks. She'd take precautions, yes, but she also planned on treasuring every moment. This might be her one and only pregnancy.

"Charlotte's right, odds are excellent for a healthy outcome," Hailey said reassuringly. "We'll make sure you stay low risk and Ty too."

"How you gonna do that?" Mad asked.

Hailey leaned around Charlotte to speak directly to Mad.

"I'm far more than just a matchmaking wedding planner. I have connections in all sorts of industries. We're going to come up with some way for Ty to have the career he loves with lower risk and we're all going to take care of Charlotte."

A tickling of unease had Charlotte speaking up. "Don't worry about Ty. I'll talk to him."

Hailey went on as if Charlotte hadn't spoken, already deep in planning mode. "We're getting Julia in on this and Claire too. I want all hands on deck!" They both used to be in book club. Julia had left when she had her daughter, Grace. Now she spent all her time taking care of Grace and writing her erotic romance novels during her daughter's naptime. Claire was absent due to her movie-star career.

Hailey grabbed her cell and went into the kitchen to talk. Charlotte really hoped Hailey wasn't doing anything too crazy. Charlotte hadn't even spoken to Ty yet. She needed him to know she wouldn't stand in his way of doing what he loved, even if it was hard on her heart. She wanted him happy most of all. Now that she thought about it, who was Ty calling?

Ten minutes later, Hailey poked her head out of the kitchen to say Julia had invited Charlotte to call or come over any time with any questions she had and even offered her mother-in-law to babysit.

"Mrs. Marino is great with kids," Missy put in. "She's my sister's mother-in-law too. She regularly has all the grandkids over at the house. You should come to Sunday dinner. I'm sure she'd love to meet you and help out."

"But I don't even know Julia's family," Charlotte said.

"Yeah, yeah, you know them," Mad put in. "Nico Marino is Park's boss. Now you're my sister, so you're practically family with them too."

Charlotte wasn't quite sure how that all made sense, but given that she had zero family she could count on, she wouldn't mind having some family in her life.

"You'd be surprised," Missy said. "The Marinos, they just take you in, make you feel like family."

"That's what my family does," Mad said, almost like it

was a competition. "You can be part of ours. As soon as Ty gets off his ass and makes it official."

Charlotte laughed. "Don't give him a hard time. I have a feeling he's already planning something."

Hailey poked her head out of the kitchen again and gestured to Charlotte. "Claire wants to talk to you."

Charlotte took the phone. "Hey, Claire, how are you? Enjoying married life?"

"I love it," Claire replied in her throaty husky voice. "If I wasn't way the hell up in Vancouver, I'd be giving you a big jumping hug right now. Congratulations! I'm so happy for you. Hailey explained what a miracle it is and it couldn't have happened to a nicer couple."

"Thank you." She was a little surprised Claire spoke so positively about Ty, since the last time she'd seen them together at her wedding, Charlotte had been furious at him.

Claire went on almost as though she'd heard Charlotte's thoughts. "Ty's a good guy. And don't let the bulky muscles and booming voice fool you, he's a mushy teddy bear under all that. You know, the night before our wedding, he brought Jake to tears with his heartfelt wishes for our future. And Jake is not a crier! It was one of those zing under-the-defenses jabs straight to the heart. I wish I'd been there. It was something like he'd always looked up to him as an older brother and as a man, and he taught him by example to follow his heart, and what a huge success Jake was in every aspect of his life. But *so* much better than that."

Charlotte smiled. "Yeah, he does that."

"I know I'm not there with you all as much as I want to be, but I'm going to do whatever I can to help."

"Thanks. I appreciate it."

"Make sure you fill out a baby registry. I'm going to get you absolutely everything on it and I won't take no for an answer."

Charlotte smiled. "Okay."

"See? You know better than to argue with me. Okay, stay strong, sister. I'll be back in Connecticut in time for your third trimester and the birth. You just found out, right? You're like, what, a month along?"

"I think so."

"Awesome. I'll be back to film *Fierce Loving* September first, and every spare moment I'll be checking in to see how awesome you're doing. Oh! I'll make some phone calls and make sure we get the best specialists lined up for you and the baby too."

"Thanks, Claire, that means a lot. More than you know." She liked her doctor but wouldn't mind knowing she had others waiting in the wings if she needed it.

"I'm so glad you're letting us in for this huge moment in your life. Believe me, I know how hard it is to let people get close. You're a lot like me that way. I'm going to talk to Jake about Ty and see what we might come up with that lowers his risk level to where we're all comfortable."

"Oh, Claire, you don't have to do that. I'll talk to him. I don't want him to feel—"

"You just relax. Your sisters got your back. Ciao!" She hung up.

Oh boy. So many people making so many plans without her. She knew it was all with good intentions, but at some point she had to wrangle them all in the same direction. She shook her head, smiling to herself. It was a good problem to have. She'd spent her whole life doing everything on her own. Now she had more than enough help. Everything would work out.

Ty appeared suddenly in front of her. "I'm staying in Connecticut until the baby is born. I just took a leave of absence."

"Yay!" She threw her arms around his neck.

"Hey, no sudden movements. Take it easy. Nice and slow back to the sofa."

She bit back a laugh, knowing his concern came from a good place. She'd educate him on pregnancy later.

16

———

That night Ty washed the dinner dishes so Charlotte could stay off her feet. Everything about this pregnancy felt fragile and delicate. He hadn't even been able to have sex earlier. Not because of Charlotte, she was all in, trying to seduce him as soon as her friends left. He called a halt to the proceedings because all he could think about was accidentally jostling the baby or poking it or something. Charlotte had laughed and said he needed some pregnancy education, which irritated him because she was just as new at all this, but then she took him in her hot mouth with the perfect amount of suction. If they had to stick to blow jobs for her safety, he'd deal.

See? He was already getting the hang of being a good husband.

He finished up, grabbed his crutches, and joined Charlotte where she was watching some reality show about a pregnant woman. He took one look at the woman—hugely pregnant and walking down a hospital hallway with an IV—and immediately felt nauseous. It was just too easy to imagine it was Charlotte. And there he'd be at the hospital, waiting, helpless, not knowing if everything was going to turn out okay. He grabbed the remote and changed the channel.

"Hey!" Charlotte protested. "It was just getting good."

The news blared and it was more than he could take right now. He shut the TV off and ran his hands down her arms, needing the reassuring touch. "What can I do to keep you safe?"

"I am safe."

He snagged her hands and squeezed. "I mean you and the baby. Safe and healthy, that's all I want."

She smiled. "You're so sweet. Everything's fine. None of the high-risk stuff happens until I'm further along. We have a few worry-free months."

That didn't cut it for the amount of anxious energy kicking through his body. He wanted to pace or run or kick someone's ass. Of course, he couldn't with a broken leg. He drummed his fingers on his thigh.

"I know what will make you feel better," she said with a note of seduction in her voice.

"I don't want a blow job right now." He shoved both hands through his hair. "I'm freaking out, if you can't tell." He'd made a bunch of phone calls, trying to piece together some kind of plan that made sense to him, but there were too many loose ends, too many uncertainties.

"You've been freaking out ever since you got here. I know it was a shock. Let me help you out." She gave him a sexy smile and started to take off her shirt.

He snagged the bottom of her shirt and pulled it back in place. "Keep it on. We're not having sex until after the baby is born and then only after the doc says you're okay."

"Seriously?" she asked in an incredulous voice.

"Seriously."

She gave him a small impish smile. "We can still hug and kiss, right?"

He eyed her suspiciously. That sounded like a gateway to heavier stuff to him.

She lifted one shoulder up and down. "Okay, we'll just hang out."

"Oh no, you can't fool me with that *just hanging out* stuff. That's my line. How do you think we got here? Just hang out is code for let's get naked."

She laughed and threw her arms around him. "I was not aware of that."

"This isn't funny! I'm...look...just stay still, okay? No sudden movements. Relax on the sofa for the rest of the pregnancy and I'll take care of everything else."

Her brows shot up. "You know I have work on Monday after the doctor's appointment."

"Baby, you're not working out. You're doing *nothing*. Absolutely nothing except growing our healthy baby."

She kissed him. "We'll talk to the doctor about it. Last time I checked, you're not a doctor."

He pulled her into his lap with a slow move, tucking her sideways against him, careful not to jostle her anywhere near her stomach.

"You don't have to treat me like I'm fragile." She squeezed him in a tight hug. "Give me one of your signature Ty hugs."

He gave her a small squeeze. "How soon can we get married?"

"As soon as Hailey can fit us in, I guess. I'm not sure what's involved with the license and all that, but she'll know. Get in touch with her; she's eager to do it. We just have to set a date and then let people know. I'm not on speaking terms with my mom, so I'll just be inviting my friends, my boss, and you, of course." She beamed. "Life is good. Let's enjoy it."

His heart slowed, feeling better at least he had this wedding part locked down. "I'll get my family there. We'll see if Claire and Jake can fly in."

"Are you okay with getting married with crutches? It'll be in all the pictures."

"I'll be in a walking boot in a couple of weeks. It's better than waiting and having you be hugely pregnant in the pictures."

"I don't mind. I'm so happy. It's my very own miracle."

"It's our miracle," he said, brushing his lips across hers. He cradled her cheek, stroking the soft skin with his thumb.

She did a little wiggle dance in his lap. "My man," she whispered, running her hands through his hair and then kissing him. He quickly decided kissing was okay and they had a hot make-out session.

Next thing he knew, she was begging him to give it to her. This *always* happened. He was an excellent kisser. He might've let his hands roam too.

He held her head with one hand. "Come on, baby, I told ya we're not going to do that for a while. I'll give you a glow job this time."

"We've been making love for weeks before I knew. Remember how hard you fucked me last time, over and over…" Her lips parted on a breathy sigh. She slowly ran her hands up her breasts, her neck, her face and through her hair. Dirty talk and touching herself, the woman was devious.

He was blue steel.

She kept going in a husky seductive voice, her hand stroking down her neck. "Up and down, taking me *so deep*."

His cock pulsed. "Okay, okay, but real gentle. Real slow. I control it."

She gave him a small smile. "Okay."

He gestured for them to move to the bedroom. Once there, they got naked in record time. He arranged her on top so he wouldn't accidentally wallop her with his cast. She let out a long sexy sigh as she took him in slowly, inch by inch. Hot bliss. He rocked her gently, keeping her sitting upright, his favorite rider. She made these sexy needy noises and he could feel his control slipping because it'd been a while since he'd had her. When he felt like he needed to thrust hard, he snagged her by the waist and tried to set her away but she hung on with her hands and strong thighs.

"All the way," she urged like a demanding cowgirl. "Give me what I need. What only you can give."

She had all the best dirty words. "That's right, baby, I give you what you need." He stroked her slick center, rocking her gently, and then increased the pressure with his fingers. She gasped.

He eased up. "Breathe normally. Steady, steady."

She grabbed his wrist and made him press harder. "Yes," she said on a moan.

He slowed down, stroking firmly the way she liked. She closed her eyes, her head tilting back as though she was relaxing into it.

"Yeah, that's right," he told her. "Nice and easy." He rocked her gently, his own pleasure increasing with her soft sigh.

She started moving faster, and the pleasure ratcheted up for both of them. He felt her tighten around him, knew she was going to go off, and stilled so he didn't instinctively thrust. He kept her still too, one hand clamped on her hip as his other hand stroked her faster and harder. He watched her face, her jaw slack, and then that beautiful moment of pure ecstasy as her body clenched around him. He felt himself grow thicker. She shuddered on a long moan and he held her through it, keeping her as still as he could, everything tightly controlled.

She slowly opened her eyes and gave him a goofy grin. "You rock."

He grinned. "I know."

"Can I move now?"

"Small controlled movements."

"Like this?" She rocked her pelvis faster than he'd let her before, and it felt so damn good, he let her.

"Yes, just like…" And then he was coming. He held her by the hips, pumping inside her, unable to control his own movements. Finally he was spent. He met her soft brown eyes. "You okay?"

She smiled. "I'm great."

He lifted her off him and carefully rolled to his side, mindful of his cast. He pulled her into his arms in a loose embrace, cupping her head to his chest. She wrapped her arms around his middle and squeezed tight.

"Give me a real hug," she said. "It's good for the baby to know how much we love each other."

He tightened his hold a little and she sighed. He stroked her hair, down her back, and then stroked from her shoulders to her wrists, needing the reassurance that everything was good with her.

He felt like his heart was walking around naked and exposed outside his body.

He wished he could tuck his heart—her—somewhere safe. Like a bubble in a beautiful meadow surrounded by medical personnel.

He was getting nuts.

"I think I'll feel better when I talk to your doctor," he said.

"I think so too." She lifted her head and met his eyes. "Oh, Ty, I've never been so happy in my life. I never thought I'd feel this way about anyone and the pregnancy just puts everything into this whole other wonderful place."

"I'm glad, me too," he said because he was happy. But he was also thinking he'd never been so scared in his entire life and he'd done plenty of risky things for his job. He tucked her head against his shoulder and held her snug against his body.

The only thing that would make him feel better was twenty-four-seven care for Charlotte. He couldn't wait to set his plan in motion on Monday after her doctor appointment. In the meantime, he'd meet with Alex tomorrow, Sunday night, to get all the details straight from the man who'd lived a risky pregnancy and paid the ultimate price.

The next night Ty was exhausted after the day he'd had trying to keep Charlotte resting. The woman was unbelievably energetic given her condition. She'd only rest naked in bed, which required huge amounts of energy from him to keep her from getting overly excited.

He propped his elbows on his dad's kitchen table and rested his head in his hands, waiting for Alex to put Viv to bed upstairs in Mad's old room. They'd met here because Alex was sure she'd fall asleep on the drive over, which made it easier to plan a meeting time. At home, bedtime was never a sure thing, a "moving target," as Alex said. It was just the three of them tonight. Their dad was out at his part-time gig as a security guard at an office park.

"Wake up," Alex said.

Ty lifted his head and smiled. "Hey, I'm awake." For the first time in a long time Ty really studied his brother to see how he was holding up under fatherhood. His dark brown hair was cropped shorter than it'd ever been before Viv, especially on the sides, like maybe he'd taken a clipper to it himself. His jaw sported at least a couple days' growth and there were dark circles under his eyes. Surprisingly he was muscular and fit. Ty could see as much from the blue T-shirt Alex wore. No gut either.

"You still working out?" Ty asked. The personal trainer in him was curious.

Alex flashed a smile. "Thanks for noticing. You want something to drink?"

"Just water."

Alex retrieved two glasses, filled them at the sink, dumped some ice in them, and joined him at the table.

"Thanks," Ty said. "When do you find time to work out with your clients and Viv?" Alex couldn't hang onto a nanny long enough to put a dent in his workload. Not entirely his fault, though his brother didn't tolerate slackers where his daughter was concerned, it was mostly because Viv was such a handful. The girl couldn't help it with the hell-on-wheels Campbell genes (so like Mad at that age) and her mom, Tammy, had been a wild free spirit, an artist like Alex was before he had to pay the bills.

"I work out with Viv," Alex said. "She's my counterweight. Twenty-six pounds and as she grows and gains more weight, my workout gradually intensifies."

"That's brilliant." A workout for parents and kids together was already cranking through Ty's brain. "I gotta see this in action."

"Four o'clock is when we rock." Alex grinned. "She just thinks it's a fun game."

"So you're using her as a free weight?"

"Yeah, I lift her a bunch of times." He demonstrated some curls. "Overhead lifts too."

"What else?"

"I put her on my back when I do push-ups, she sits on my feet for stomach crunches, and then I shift her to my lower legs and lift her that way too. Plus we dance."

"You dance?" Who knew the Campbell brothers were dancers? Ty had picked it right up with the help of a professional choreographer, but he'd only ever seen Alex do a slow shuffle.

Alex took a drink. "Yup. Just for the aerobic benefits." He chuckled. "That's her favorite part. She calls it dance party and, boy, does she get loud." At Ty's puzzled look, Alex added, "She sings really loud. Like earsplitting."

"What's she singing?" He hoped it wasn't Alex's music, alternative, edgy stuff with lyrics that weren't appropriate for a two-year-old.

A faint blush crept up Alex's neck. "So I hear congrats are in order. You psyched?"

"I'm scared shitless."

"Why?"

"She's high risk. Best I can explain it is a lot of scar tissue was removed from inside her and that can cause problems both for her and the baby."

"Oh, shit."

"Yeah. The doc only gave her a one percent chance of even getting pregnant."

"Man, you got the power sperm, huh?"

He couldn't even joke about it. That was how freaked he was. He rattled off all the risks that were never far from his mind. "She might need a C-section, she might hemorrhage, the baby might come too early." He shoved a hand in his hair. "What was it like for you and Tammy? Did you know there was a lot of risk for her ahead of time?"

Alex's lips formed a flat line. He was quiet for so long that Ty was about to tell him to forget it, when Alex finally spoke, staring at the table. "Tammy wasn't high risk at all. Everything went so smoothly with the pregnancy. She was perfectly healthy." Alex rubbed the back of his neck. "I wanted to marry her right away, as soon as we heard she was pregnant, but she wanted to wait until after Viv was born."

"I know," Ty said softly. "You don't have to talk about it if it's too hard."

"No, it's okay. It's been two years." Alex finally lifted his head, his brown eyes watery, which made Ty's eyes water in sympathy. "Things started going south during the labor and then suddenly the baby's heart rate was dropping. They wanted to do a C-section immediately. They had to put her under general anesthesia, which is riskier, but there wasn't time for an epidural. She'd never been under before." He cleared his throat. "It's a common procedure; usually things go fine. It's rare what happened to her." Alex looked in the distance as though he was remembering that moment. "I was there, right there in the operating room. Viv's taken out, she's good, she's healthy. I'm so happy. And then Tammy, her body just shut down. The monitors are going crazy, beeping and blaring; her heart stopped. They tried to revive her. I was right there, watching her die."

"I'm so sorry," Ty said.

"She never got to see Viv." His eyes, hooded with grief, met Ty's. "Can you imagine?"

Ty shook his head, his eyes stinging with tears of sympathy, but he sat quietly, giving Alex the space he needed to talk. He wasn't sure if his brother had ever shared all the details with anyone before. It was the first he was hearing of it.

"There was nothing I could do," Alex said, his voice hollow. "Nothing anyone could do. It was a good hospital, good doctors; it was just the risk of surgery. Any surgery."

Ty clapped a hand on his brother's shoulder.

Alex nodded a silent thanks and took another drink of water. "Guess I'm not much help."

"I'm glad you told me." Shit happened was what it came down to, even for a low-risk situation.

"How do you manage it all?" Ty finally asked as the reality of Alex being both mom and dad hit home. He hadn't thought too much about it, honestly. He knew their dad helped out a lot with Viv, and Alex seemed so natural with her like he instinctively knew what to do. It must've been tough. Ty had been on the other side of the country and hadn't seen his brother doing the daddy thing all that much.

"I manage because I have to," Alex said simply.

Ty lowered his voice, almost afraid to ask his next question, but needing to know in case it went down like that for him. "How were you able to go on after you lost Tammy and then suddenly you have this baby?"

"Daddy!" Viv hollered.

Alex stood. "That's how. She needs me; I'm there." He strode out of the room.

Ty followed at a slower pace on crutches. Alex scooped Viv up where she was already halfway down the stairs in her blue pajamas with a pink dinosaur graphic. Her wavy light brown hair was messy, her cheeks pink. "Where's your socks?" Alex asked.

Viv pointed upstairs. Alex carried Viv in one arm back upstairs, retrieved the socks from the hallway with the other arm, carried her down, and stopped, slipping the socks back on one-handed. Viv rested her head on Alex's shoulder, stuck her thumb in her mouth, and twirled her hair. Alex was her everything.

"Let's go," Alex said to Ty. "I need to get her home tucked in her own bed for the night."

Ty followed him out the door.

"And don't worry so much," Alex said on the way to his car. "Just deal the hand you're dealt. You'll figure stuff out on the way. Not saying it's easy, but…you manage."

Ty felt the truth of that in his bones. Still he knew he'd never look at Alex the same way again. Now he was alert to every little thing Alex did with Viv from buckling her into her booster seat to the way he talked to her, whether or not she answered, as he covered her with a small yellow fleece blanket.

"You're my new hero," Ty said once Alex was in the car.

Alex barked out a laugh. "Yeah, okay, just don't look behind the curtain."

17

Monday's doctor appointment had Ty breathing easier. Charlotte had been right; her chances were good for a healthy pregnancy. She was even okay for continuing to work out in these early months with some precautions, which she swore to Ty she would take. After the doctor's appointment, Charlotte drove him to the garage where Park worked for the next part of his plan. He couldn't drive with his right leg in a cast. Fortunately, she didn't have to go to work until late afternoon. He'd told her to wait in the car because he'd only be a few minutes, but really he just wanted her off her feet. He knew it didn't make sense. She was going to work after this, but he felt the need to protect her when he was with her. He had to do something as the daddy and future husband.

Park wiped his hands on a rag and stepped out of the four-bay garage, where he'd been working on a red Ferrari Dino. "Hey, what're you doing here?"

Ty moved in closer to the car. "This is a beauty. Early seventies?"

Park grinned. "Nineteen seventy-two 246 GT Dino Coupe. One owner. She's going to fetch a pretty penny at auction."

Ty nodded, even happier to hear Park speak car than usual. "How're you doing? They treat you well around here?"

He glanced over to the parking lot to make sure Charlotte was still in the car, relaxing as he'd told her to.

"Can't complain," Park said. "I've got awesome projects. Nico over there—" he tilted his head toward a dark-haired Italian man retrieving a tool before disappearing under the hood of another Ferrari "—knows everything classic cars." He lowered his voice. "He owns the place."

"Introduce us," Ty said.

Park headed over and Ty followed. "Nico, my friend Ty asked to meet you."

Nico straightened, pulling a rag from his coveralls pocket and wiping his hands before shaking Ty's hand. "Nice to meet you, Ty. You looking for a classic car?"

Ty shook his head. "Actually not just yet. I need a tank to keep my lady safe. She's pregnant."

Nico flashed a smile that even Ty had to admit was movie-star quality. "Congrats. Best thing in the world. I've got a twenty-one-month-old daughter, Chloe, and another on the way. Wife thinks it's another girl, but my money's on a boy. Lotta boys in our family."

Ty laughed. "Yeah, ours too. I don't know what we're having, but as long as it's healthy—"

"Yeah, absolutely," Nico said.

"Great place you got here," Ty said, gesturing to the garage and the attached showroom.

"Thanks," Nico said, looking at him expectantly.

Ty got down to business. "You ever think about a reality show about what you all do here?" He needed a paying gig that kept him near Charlotte at least until the baby was born. Most of his money was tied up in his house in LA, where he hoped they'd live once the baby arrived. He figured if things worked out with a reality show, he could fit it into his schedule between stunt-work gigs.

Park stared at Ty, jaw dropped. Maybe Ty should've mentioned the idea to Park first.

Nico grimaced. "You mean a TV show?"

"Yeah," Ty said, pumping enthusiasm into his voice. "Like

the cameras follow you when you find a classic car and then show the before and after of it being restored."

Nico shook his head. "I have zero interest in being on TV."

"It could be good for business," Ty said. "National coverage. People would come from all over to buy classic cars from you. My brother could set up a website too, where people could shop online." Alex was a graphic designer with multiple projects, including designing websites.

Nico seemed to be considering it.

Ty rushed on. "It wouldn't cost you a dime. My sister-in-law is Claire Jordan. She'd run it through her production company." That was the next part of his plan, but he needed Nico and Park on board first.

Nico nodded. "I know Claire. She made the movies out of my sister-in-law Julia's books. The Fierce trilogy. I was an extra in one scene." He shuddered. "So damn boring that line of work."

"Yeah, that's her," Ty said. "You wouldn't have to be on camera if you didn't want. Maybe we could just do it for Park's projects." He hitched a thumb at Park.

"This your idea?" Nico asked Park.

"This is all news to me," Park said.

Ty barreled on. "I'll be the personality and Park will be the technical know-how. I'm a stuntman and I work in front of the camera all the time."

Park held up a hand. "Whoa, Ty, I've never been on TV. I'm sure I'd bore the viewers to tears."

Ty clapped him on the back. "Nah. When you talk cars, you're interesting."

"Thanks a lot," Park said drily.

Nico chuckled.

Ty turned to Nico. "Think about it. It could be a real boon to business. If it's okay with you, I'll run it by Claire and have her get in touch to work out the details. You'd be compensated for any inconvenience. I'm sure we could get you some kind of consultant fee or percentage or something."

"I'll think about it," Nico said and went back to work.

"Can I tell Claire about the idea?" Ty called to Nico's retreating back.

Nico stopped and turned. "Sure. But nothing's definite until I see the terms all in black and white. My wife's a lawyer; I want her eyes on it."

Ty would've done a victory jump and whoop if he wasn't in a cast. "Thank you so much," he said instead.

Nico grunted and went back under the hood.

Ty gestured for Park to follow him outside. As soon as they got there, Park said, "Where did you get this crazy idea?" He lowered his voice. "And you might have mentioned it to me before telling my boss."

"Sorry, you're right. I'm freaking out about Charlotte. I need a gig that'll keep me near her. Who else would I want to work with than you, my main man, my bro—"

"All right, shut up." Park socked him on the shoulder. "You know I'd do anything for family."

Park was not only engaged to Ty's sister, Mad, but also his honorary brother since Ty's dad took him in at ten years old. No one he'd rather do business with than Park, an honorable and hardworking guy. Plus Park's deep reserve would play well on camera, balancing Ty's natural put-it-all-out-there enthusiasm.

Park glanced over Ty's shoulder toward the parking lot. "Looks like your lady missed you."

Ty turned to where Charlotte was stepping out of the car. "We're heading back," he called to Charlotte. "Stay put. I'll be right there." She sat again and shut the door. He breathed a sigh of relief. It was going to take a while for him to truly relax about her high-risk status.

"Congrats, by the way," Park said. "Mad told me it's a miracle baby."

"Thanks, but it's not a sure thing yet. She's high risk and I need to keep a close eye on her." He glanced over his shoulder at Charlotte tapping her fingers on the steering wheel. "I'd better go. Think about it."

Park clapped him on the shoulder and squeezed. "You work out the details and I'll see what I can do on this end."

"Thanks, I owe you."

"Don't think I won't collect," Park said with a grin.

Ty made his way back to Charlotte as quickly as he could on crutches.

"You buying a car?" Charlotte asked when he got in the car.

"I am, but not here. I want something new and big like a tank." Now he was even looking at cars in a whole new light, for their safety instead of their power, speed, and coolness factor.

"A tank?"

"Yeah, whadda ya call it, a van or something. Maybe a Hummer."

"Okay," she said slowly.

As soon as they got back to Charlotte's house, he escorted her safely to the sofa and put on the TV, telling her he was making her a healthy lunch before she went to work. But first he needed to make a phone call. He crossed right through the kitchen and out to the small backyard. He didn't want to reveal any of the details of his plan to Charlotte until he was sure it would work. No use in getting her riled up over nothing.

He called Claire and actually got her. "Hey, it's your favorite brother-in-law."

"Hi, Josh," she said warmly. "How are you?"

"It's Ty."

She laughed her famous throaty husky laugh. "I know. I've got the whole Campbell clan programmed into my phone. How's our girl?"

"She's good. Listen, I have an idea that might help me be here for her more."

"Anything," Claire said. "I love her like my own flesh and blood."

He got a chill at the intensity in her voice, even over the phone. "I'm thinking a reality show about classic cars. I'd be the host; Park would do the technical nitty-gritty. Your production company would run it. The place where Park works is locally well known for the quality and variety of classic cars. I ran it by the owner and he's open to hearing more."

"I'll pitch it to the Turbo channel. They're all cars all the time. If not, I'll try PBS. Worst case, we'll create a series of webisodes. Hold on."

He did a silent fist pump that she was on board so fast.

A few moments later, Claire said, "Jake wants to back it as his first producer credit. I'll get you and Park on payroll with health insurance for you. Give me the number of the car place and I'll work out something with the owner too."

A huge weight lifted off his shoulders. "Yes to all of that. How can I thank you?"

"Wrap things up in LA and then do whatever you have to do to get back to Charlotte ASAP."

"I'm on it." His eyes watered at the caring Claire showed for their situation. "Claire, you have my undying support forever. Really. Anything you need, *ever*, I'll do it. I'm so glad you're in our family."

"Now you're going to make me cry. Geez. You Campbells are so damn expressive. I love you too." She sniffled and took a deep breath. "Okay, I'm okay. Now I want you to be aware of all possible outcomes for your show. We're going to start with a pilot episode. That's what I'm going to pitch. If it doesn't work, if you and Park have zero chemistry, or maybe you do and we get the deal, but no one tunes in, I want you to be thinking of a plan B. Got it?"

He already was, contingencies upon contingencies rattling through his brain. "Got it."

He hung up, quickly put together a healthy salad and sandwich for him and Charlotte, and brought lunch out to the coffee table.

Charlotte smiled. "What're you so busy planning, Ty? You're acting very strange. Tell me what's going on."

"I'm planning stuff for our wedding to surprise you." He sat next to her and pointed to her lunch. "Now eat."

"Really?" She took a bite of turkey sandwich. "I thought Hailey was taking care of all that."

"I'm helping." He ate his sandwich, watching in his peripheral vision that she was doing okay.

"You can relax. I feel great. Nothing's going to happen to me."

His gut clenched and he put his sandwich down. That was exactly what he'd told her, "nothing's going to happen to me," expecting the words to be enough to ease her worries about the risks he took, but now he knew on a gut level that nothing would ever make him feel better about her being high risk. He'd seen the aftermath of the worst-case scenario with Alex and he couldn't shake the terror of the same thing happening to them.

She gave him a look of sympathy and set her sandwich down, taking his hand. "Really. Nothing's going to happen to me. Just like nothing's going to happen to you with your stunts. After your leave of absence, once the baby's here, it's okay with me if you go back to it. I know I was freaking out before, but I don't want you to give up your dream job for me. I don't want you to resent me or the baby or feel like you're missing out. I just want you to be happy."

He stared at her, shocked to hear it. "Really? But you were so worried before."

She cupped his face and gazed into his eyes with so much love he got choked up before she said a word. "I love you so much that I put no conditions on it. I love you so much that all I want is for you to have everything you want."

"So you want me to keep my job?"

She lifted her palms. "I want you to do what makes you happy."

"Good."

"Okay, that's settled, then." She gave him a small smile and he saw in her eyes what it cost her to give him that.

"Char, I just want you to know how much it means that you're making this sacrifice for my happiness. I know it's hard on you. And, well, that's how much I love you too. I quit."

Her eyes widened. "What do you mean you quit?"

"I mean my leave of absence is permanent. No more stunt

work. I'm selling my house in LA and I'm staying here with you permanently."

Her hand flew to her mouth. "When did you decide all this?"

"Just now."

She let out a happy cry. "Ty, are you sure?"

He nodded. "The moment I heard you were high risk, I understood how you felt. You can't help being high risk and it's because you're carrying my baby. *I* can help it."

"But what will you do? Mad says you hated being a personal trainer."

"I didn't hate it. I was restless. Then again I was twenty at the time. Things are different now with you and the baby."

"But now you're sacrificing for my happiness," she protested. "I don't want you to regret it."

He wrapped his arms around her in a gentle hug. "No regrets. I'm jumping in with both feet, eyes wide open." Her shoulders shook and he pulled back to see she was crying. The doctor said she'd be extra emotional with all the pregnancy hormones. He tipped her chin up and kissed her gently on the lips and cheek and jaw and back to her luscious mouth, trying to make her feel better.

He wiped her tears with his thumbs. "Better?"

She nodded and kissed him again. He obliged, always willing to do his part in making her feel better and better and better.

Things got out of hand.

They always seemed to with Charlotte. He really couldn't help it if she found him irresistible. He understood. She was irresistible too.

18

Two weeks later, Charlotte was feeling pretty good about life. The doctor was optimistic (with a few cautionary warnings about symptoms that required an immediate call), she had no morning sickness, and best of all, Ty was on board one hundred percent. He'd quit his job, which she was happy about, but of course she would've liked it better if he'd had a job to replace it before he quit. She'd have to scale back at work in a few months.

"Dinner," Ty called from the kitchen.

"Coming!" She smiled to herself at the wonder of the man in her kitchen. He didn't want her on her feet any more than was necessary and had taken over cooking and washing dishes. Who was she to complain? She'd been doing all that for herself for most of her life and it was nice to be treated so special, even if it was a little over the top.

"Smells delicious," she said, stepping into the kitchen. It was his Monday night specialty, spaghetti and store-bought meatballs. She crossed to where he was piling spaghetti on a plate and kissed his cheek. He was off crutches now and wearing a walking boot.

He smiled. "Bring your plate to the living room. I want you to watch something on TV."

"Sure." She let him finish adding everything, snagged

both plates, and headed to the living room. Ty followed with tall glasses of milk. He made sure she had enough protein for the baby's growth. He actually read all the info on the pregnancy websites she'd sent him.

Ty loaded a DVD and grabbed the remote to get it started. "Ready?" he asked with a grin.

"What're we watching?"

"You'll see." He pressed play.

Ty appeared on the screen in a black T-shirt and black jeans, looking edgy and sexy, talking right into the camera. The jeans covered his walking boot and, honestly, it just added to his slow swagger.

"What is this!" she exclaimed.

"Shh, listen," he said with a wide smile. "And eat."

She did. Ty on screen sounded so relaxed and natural. "Classic cars are a high-stakes game. Who will discover the ultimate barn find? And what'll it be worth after it's restored? That's the name of the game at Exotic and Classic Restorations. I'm here with Nico Marino, owner of the shop, who found this nineteen fifty-six Jaguar XK140SE Roadster in an abandoned garage." The type of car appeared in bold on the bottom of the screen. "Tell us more about the car."

Nico obliged, moving around the car to point out its features.

The camera zoomed in on Ty again. "Chief mechanic, Parker Shaw, will be bringing this car to its former glory. We're hoping it'll bring six figures at auction. Let's see how it all pans out."

"Park too?" she exclaimed.

Ty squeezed her hand. "Yeah."

She watched as Ty talked up the car and the history of its kind, his own enthusiasm contagious, even for someone like her who didn't know much about cars. Then there were some shots of Park working on the car and explaining what he was doing. Park and Ty took it for a test drive and then sold it at auction for a primo price. At the end, Park and Ty had a lightning round of questions, testing each other's car knowledge, that had her laughing. They were both knowledgeable; it was just fun to watch them try to one up each other and rib each other for a close but not quite answer.

The episode ended, and Ty turned to her. "What do you think?"

"It was awesome! Fun, informative, and entertaining. When did you do all this?"

"Two weeks of early mornings to get it together."

"That's where you went early mornings? I thought you were working out."

"Nope. And I wanted to wait until we were further along before getting your hopes up."

"It's awesome."

He waved toward the screen. "Honestly, the auction was for another car. We edited it in just as an example. We'll have a theme song and some catchy title too. Claire's still working on that part."

Her jaw dropped. "You and Claire put this together? Is that what all those phone calls were about?"

"Yeah. Some of them. The show will mostly be me and Park. Nico will only do the initial car intro. Claire convinced him it would be good for business. You know, the man behind the name. She told him it was because of his expertise, but she told me it was because he was eye candy." He gave her side eye, waiting for her reaction.

"Oh, no! You're definitely the eye candy on this show." *Though Nico was very easy on the eyes.*

Ty gave a small nod, seeming satisfied with her answer. "If it goes well, this is my new job and we're filming in Connecticut. Maybe a few field trips to pick up a classic car, but otherwise I'm here. Jake's producing it through Claire's company."

"I can't believe you guys put all this together and I had no idea!"

"I wanted to surprise you." He kissed her and pulled her into his lap in one smooth motion. "It's low risk and pays well. I'll be so close to you, you'll be dying to get me out of your hair." He stroked her hair and wrapped it around his fist, tilting her head back for his kiss.

She spoke as soon as he let her up for air. "I'll never want you out of my hair."

He grinned. "The best part is, it'll only film in the spring and summer when the weather's good. The rest of the year I'm all yours. Maybe we can build our own personal training business here. I take the clients when you're on maternity leave, and then you pick up with them when you're able."

"You figured it all out, didn't you?"

"Of course I did."

"You're amazing." She peppered him with kisses all over his face and neck. "If it's a boy, we'll name him Ty Jr. Only *you* could have done all of this. He's your legacy."

Ty's chest puffed out and then a moment later deflated. "Wait, you don't know my real name, do you?"

"Tyler, right?"

He held up a hand. "Okay, don't laugh."

"Uh-oh."

"I was very active in the womb."

"Not surprised."

He grimaced. "Tyger with a y."

"Tyger? Who does that to a kid?"

"My mom apparently. And, of course, there's Tiger Woods. He was setting records on the golf course while she was pregnant with me."

"But that's not his real name." She giggled. "I can't believe I haven't heard the guys teasing you about it."

Ty put his hand on her belly, as he often did like he was trying to connect with the baby. "It reminds them of my mom, so no one mentions it."

She got serious. "Sorry. I know your mom isn't your favorite. We could just call him Ty, nice and short."

His lips curled in a tender smile. "You must really love me."

"I do."

"Let's make it official, then." He reached in his pocket, took her hand, and slid a marquis-cut diamond ring on her finger.

She stared at it. "Oh, Ty, it's so beautiful."

He cradled her face with one hand and gazed into her eyes. "Saturday. All planned. You just show up with the dress. Zero stress for my woman."

She threw her arms around his neck. "Perfect."

On Saturday Ty surprised her yet again. She thought for sure when he said he planned a wedding that he'd left it mostly to Hailey, which meant a wedding in Clover Park at Ludbury House, where Hailey hosted most weddings, but no. Not at all.

It was on a yacht tied to a dock right off of Connecticut's shore. The very same boat they'd gotten stranded in the mud for their magical first date where they revealed so much of who they were on the inside. Except this time the captain, not Ty, the real captain, actor and comedian Will McKay, was in charge.

All of her friends were there, even Claire had flown in and brought her stylist to do everyone's hair and makeup at Charlotte's house. Hailey had taken care of the dress, taking Charlotte shopping in a boutique she knew well that gave them the red-carpet treatment. Her dress was a curve-hugging white satin with a straight strapless neckline and a small train. A long veil trailed down her back. She *loved* it. All of it.

Her friends downplayed their part in making Charlotte's wedding so stress-free. In fact, the first thing Claire said upon arrival was, "Don't blame me for your overbearing fiancé. He's the one bossing everyone around, arranging for your bridal needs, your honeymoon, pulling strings to get appointments with the best doctors in the city."

Charlotte had thanked both Claire and Hailey profusely anyway, knowing it was Claire's pull as a celebrity and Hailey's organized efficiency that made Ty's plans come together.

Now it was near sunset and the wedding reception was still going strong. Claire checked in with Charlotte to make sure she was happy with everything. Hailey rushed over to repeat the question and reminded Charlotte the wedding cake was the healthy kind, carrot cake, and really not her fault. Ty insisted on it for the baby.

"It's okay," Charlotte said. "I love everything." She took both of them in, emotion making her throat tight and her eyes water. "I love you, you're my sisters."

"Sisters from another mister," Claire put in.

Hailey nodded vigorously, her own eyes watering.

"Hey, what are we, chopped worm guts?" Mad hollered.

"Get over here!" Charlotte hollered back.

Mad snagged Lauren by the arm, who snagged Carrie. Hailey hurried to gather up the rest of the Happy Endings Book Club ladies from where they mingled. A crazy commotion of hugging and exclaiming followed until Ty came over to make sure Charlotte wasn't getting jostled.

"Easy, ladies," Ty said. "Excuse us, it's time for our slow dance. They're playing our song."

"'SexyBack' is our song?" Charlotte asked.

Ty quirked a brow. "You have to ask?"

"Bit on the nose, isn't it?" Mad asked.

"Blame Charlotte," Ty said. "This is her favorite song. She asked me to dance to it before she'd agree to go out with me." He turned to Charlotte. "Own it, baby."

"Ty!" Charlotte exclaimed. "It's not my favorite."

Ty kissed her. "It's mine because it got me you."

"Oh, Ty." She threw her arms around him, hugging him tight. He was so damn sweet. He returned the hug in a restrained gentle way before taking her hand and guiding her toward the large back deck. Her friends whistled and hollered, "Sexy, sexy!" behind her.

"You know I'm never going to live this down," she told him, walking behind him on the narrow path to the back deck.

"I'm sure we'll give them lots more stuff to talk about in the future," he said, tossing a wicked grin over his shoulder. She shook her head at him, smiling.

Ty was still in the walking boot, so he couldn't dance much at the reception, except for the slow dances, which he was happy about because he didn't want her to dance. He was adamant that she not "shake things up in there." She agreed as long as they could still have a honeymoon with full naked privileges. They would have it in the penthouse of a gorgeous exclusive hotel nearby in the city, where Claire had connections.

They arrived on the back deck and Ty pulled her into his arms, dancing cheek to cheek, barely moving despite the faster-paced song.

"Sure is a different sunset-cruise experience this time around," she said.

"Smells a helluva lot better too," he returned with a chuckle.

"And you're fully dressed in a tux," she said. "I think I liked the towel and flimsy robe look better. Such a shame to hide that gorgeous body."

He nuzzled her neck and whispered in her ear, "Won't be hidden for long, baby. Can't wait for our honeymoon."

"Me too."

His voice was a husky promise. "I'm gonna gently rock your world."

She couldn't help her smile. "You always do."

They were the only people dancing, but she didn't mind, completely comfortable with both the company and her man. Most of the playlist were low-key slow songs at Ty's request. He was thorough in looking out for her and the baby, she'd give him that.

The guys—the Campbell brothers and friends—were nearby, talking up Will McKay for details on what the yacht could do. Except for Alex, who held Viv in a life jacket near the railing, where she pointed, oohing and aahing over the other boats in the water.

It was nothing like Charlotte ever thought her wedding would be—on a boat, pregnant with a groom who hosted a reality TV show—yet it was her perfect happy ending.

EPILOGUE

Charlotte's pregnancy was rough. Not just for her, for Ty too. His empathy for her made him overbearing at times, but always with the best of intentions. At six months along, she was put on full bed rest. Ty arranged for a nurse for when he couldn't be there and her friends rotated shifts visiting her. And while it was tough to remain resting, especially with her previously active lifestyle, she always reminded herself of the end goal—her little miracle.

But that wasn't the only miracle. For her, it was also the unexpected closeness she found once she opened up to her friends. She could honestly say they were like family. And of course, Ty's family was hers now too. Their refrigerator and freezer were stuffed with healthy meals either prepared by their family or brought over from Garner's.

Hailey even arranged for the book club to meet in Charlotte's bedroom, everyone piling on the bed with her or on folding chairs Ty had bought for visitors. Ty had sat in on the first meeting in a chair next to her side of the bed, anxious to be sure Charlotte wasn't crowded or too tired or overly excited. He told everyone he was there because he was romance-curious and had even read the book *Highlander's Mission*. He wasn't shy about contributing to the discussion either.

"Do you think Brianna would've married the man picked for her at birth if Roan hadn't survived the battle?" Ty asked right away.

The women were too busy giggling and whispering to answer. Charlotte nearly asked him to fetch her a snack or water or something, embarrassed on his behalf, but Ty was not at all embarrassed.

"Simmer down," he said. "Guys like romance too. Why do you think I fell so hard for this beauty?" He took Charlotte's hand and kissed the back of it, gazing into her eyes.

She sighed a swoony sigh. So did everyone else.

Soon they were all discussing the book, Ty included.

"What's up with Fiona anyway?" he asked. "You think she'll be with Brianna's brother in the next book? Is there a next book?"

"Yes!" Hailey said excitedly from where she sat on Ty's other side. "It's a trilogy. I'll email you the link. It's called *Highlander's Mate*."

"Is it Fiona?" Charlotte asked.

Hailey waved that away. "You'll see when we get to it. Back to *Highlander's Mission*."

Ty was happy to do so. "Can you believe Roan just moved Brianna into his fortress? I mean, he's clan leader, supposed to marry another who's about to visit, and there she is."

"Mistresses were quite common at the time," Hailey replied. "I would never tolerate it, but those were different times." She took in the group. "Dating and marriage are so much better nowadays, right, ladies?"

An animated debate over the topic ensued, which Ty listened to in rapt fascination. He'd probably never heard so many women speak so openly about the many ways men sucked. Not her man, of course, Charlotte was one of the lucky ones.

"That's why I take my job as a love facilitator so serious-ly," Hailey said. "Anyone tired of the dating scene—" she scanned the group "—please let me know and I'm happy to work my magic for your very own happy ending."

"What kind of magic?" Ty wanted to know.

"Oh, I get couples together," Hailey said.

"You do?" Ty asked, clearly surprised to hear this.

"Sure do!" Hailey beamed and then ticked them off on her fingers. "Julia and Angel, Claire and Jake, Mad and Park, and you and Charlotte."

Not one of the ladies contradicted Hailey because, in her way, she had helped things along, even if she wasn't *directly* responsible for the happy couplings.

"Me and Charlotte?" Ty echoed, his brows drawing together. "I think *I* had something to do with that."

Charlotte hid a smile.

Hailey was too polite to argue, instead turning to Mad. "Tell him."

Mad rolled her eyes and then said in a monotone, "She's the love junkie. She makes love bloom."

Charlotte patted Ty's arm. "It's on her professional wedding planner business card."

Ty gave Hailey a slow devious smile. "Maybe you can work your magic on my beast of a brother. That scoundrel. That cad." Those were Hailey's preferred names for Josh. He always called her princess in return.

Hailey flushed pink, cleared her throat, and announced briskly, "Back to Roan and Brianna. Let's stay on topic, people."

Ty chuckled. The rest of them knew better than to laugh at Hailey's expense. Hailey's evil-genius abilities had recently become abundantly clear in her dealings with her arch nemesis. Josh must be planning something truly devious in return.

After that first meeting, Ty left the rest of the meetings to just the ladies, but he still read the books. He always wanted to talk to Charlotte about them and had a lot of new ideas for them in the bedroom too, once the baby was born.

Happily, Ty Jr. was born strong and healthy, only a month early. They called him T.J.

The doctor said Charlotte's chances of getting pregnant again were still very small and the same high risk would apply. She and Ty decided to be content with the miracle they had. Neither of them wanted to risk not being there for T.J.

Ty jumped into fatherhood with both feet. It was the way he approached everything in life. Charlotte appreciated that about him and decided to apply the same gusto to her own life. As soon as T.J. was old enough, she was going to look for some studio space and open her own personal training business, working one-on-one with clients on her own schedule. For the first time in her life, she looked forward to the future with great hope and an open heart. Hard to believe it all started with a dance.

One missed dance.

One super-sexy dance.

One *let's hang out* dance.

And one slow and tender wedding dance that promised forever.

P.S. Want more Ty and Charlotte? Check out the Bonus Epilogue included in this book!

BONUS EPILOGUE

A peek into the future…

Ty carefully took his newborn daughter out of her car seat, tucked her in the cradle of his arm, and headed for the front door. No infant carrier for her. Just like with T.J., they wanted a lot of holding time with their kiddos either in their arms or in a sling. Charlotte was already ahead of him, holding two-year-old T.J. by the hand because the boy was a helluva runner. The baby was sleeping. It had been a long day; he and Charlotte had flown down to Louisiana the moment they got the call the birth mom had gone into labor. They'd spent a few days there, finished up all the paperwork, flew home and then picked up T.J. from his grandfather's house.

"Yay! Play!" T.J. exclaimed the minute they stepped inside, jumping and reaching for the baby's hand.

"Not yet," Charlotte said. "You need to give her some time to grow before you can play with her."

Ty took the baby upstairs to the nursery. Charlotte had a blast decorating for a girl—the furniture and walls were white with pops of pink color in the bedding, nursery glider chair, curtains, and area rug. Everything was coordinated and matching like in a magazine. He let her go nuts because she hadn't had a chance to do all that with T.J. since she'd been on bed rest.

T.J. ran in with a Hot Wheels car in each hand, making his loud car noises. Ty caught him just before he tried to stick the cars through the bars of the crib. He scooped up T.J., turned on the baby monitor, and carried him out. "You and me'll play, little man. Mackenzie needs her sleep so she can grow and be big enough to play with you."

T.J. ran his car up Ty's chest with a loud *vroom*!

Baby Mackenzie slept through all the noise. Already she fit right in. Even though Mackenzie was adopted, Ty couldn't help but think the little girl resembled Charlotte a bit. She had a shock of dark brown hair, brown eyes, and light tan skin. Beautiful.

He set T.J. down in the family room, who immediately shot his cars across the hardwood floor in a race before running over to the small indoor trampoline with a handle and jumping crazy high.

Their house was all set up for fitness. Little T.J. had a ton of energy, and when they couldn't take him outside, they let him loose inside. They were in a new bigger house, a four-bedroom colonial in Eastman, not far from his dad's house, who they visited regularly. Ty and Park filmed three months of the year, three days a week for their show *Hot Finds* on the Turbo Channel. The rest of the time he helped Charlotte run her personal training business in a separate studio behind the house. He worked some on the business side and jumped in with a few clients of his own too.

Charlotte had grown close to his niece Viv, inviting her over to play with T.J. regularly on the weekends, giving Viv's daddy and stepmom some couple time.

He turned on the baby monitor downstairs and then settled on the sofa, where Charlotte was slumped, eyes closed. He pushed her hair back from her face and kissed her cheek.

"How're you holding up?" he asked.

She shifted, settling her head in his lap and stretching her long legs out on the sofa. "Tired but happy."

He stroked her hair. "Me too. You think T.J. understands how long he'll have to wait to play with her?"

She closed her eyes. "No. His sense of time is the length of a *Sesame Street* episode."

This was true. Whenever they told T.J. he had to wait, he asked, "One *Sesame Street*? Two?"

Charlotte went on in a weary voice. "I don't think telling him he has to wait for at least three hundred sixty-five episodes of *Sesame Street* will mean much. One a day, of course."

Ty laughed. "Yeah, and he'll probably want to watch them all right away."

"Yup. Get it out of the way." She yawned. "We'll have to keep a close eye on him so he doesn't give her choking hazards to play with or try to pick her up or something. She's got that soft spot. Just never take your eyes off him."

His gaze shot automatically to his son. Shit. He wasn't on the trampoline. In the silence, he heard T.J. whispering through the baby monitor.

"Get up." He pushed Charlotte upright, took the stairs two at a time, and nearly sprinted to the baby's room. Charlotte wasn't far behind.

He stopped short in the doorway and signaled to Charlotte to be quiet. T.J.'s arm was in the crib, holding the baby's hand, and he was talking to her softly in his half babble way. He was just starting to string together sentences and all of his Rs, Ls, and Ss were only intelligible to people who knew him well.

"Cars and apples," T.J. said earnestly. "TV, *babble, babble,* cars." His voice rose to normal volume by the time he got to cars a second time. It was hard for him to contain his enthusiasm on the topic. They let him watch Ty's car show and it had made a huge impression. The boy was obsessed with cars.

Ty exchanged a grin with Charlotte at his side.

T.J. went on. "Mommy, cheese, *babble, babble,* Santa."

Charlotte beamed. "I came before cheese," she whispered.

"Shh," he whispered back. "I didn't hear me yet. I think I'm after Santa."

"Tree," T.J. said. "Cars, Daddy, cars, ice cream, good boy. Good girl, good girl."

Charlotte squeezed his hand. Okay, so he came after cars, apples, TV, Mommy, cheese, Santa, and a tree, but hey, he still made the cut. Before ice cream, even. Nothing like a kid to keep you humble.

He pulled Charlotte in front of him, wrapping his arms around her from behind as they watched their son introduce their daughter to the world. It was really sweet until T.J. got sleepy.

"Nap," T.J. said and started to climb the crib. Charlotte grabbed him lightning quick. T.J. yelped, probably thinking his mom had superpowers the way she always anticipated his moves. The baby slept on.

T.J. struggled mightily to get down. "Nap! Baby!"

"She's too little for that." Charlotte shifted him and tucked him tight against her, chest to chest. "You nap with Mommy."

T.J. immediately relaxed, his hand tangling in her long hair, his head resting on her shoulder. Charlotte took him to the glider, rocking gently and singing a lullaby.

Ty's heart filled to bursting at the beautiful sight of mother and son. He imagined T.J. really needed his mom after they'd been away and brought a new baby home. Ty had only vague memories of his own mom, who'd left when he was only six never to return. It gave him such pride to know his own children had an awesome mom in Charlotte.

He crossed to them, leaned down to give Charlotte a kiss and then kissed his son's chubby cheek, resting his hand on his head. He gazed at his sleeping daughter only a few feet away and let out a deep sigh of satisfaction.

Now their family was complete.

Dear Readers,

What do you think? Is Josh planning something devious for evil genius Hailey or is he too distracted watching her pretty behind for her? Maybe peacemaker Lauren can help smooth things out between the two. Or she might be too busy. After all, she's recently agreed to let Hailey find her love. Of course, that will have to be a strictly weekend endeavor because there's a tired single dad who needs her help with his little girl during the week. Next up is Alex and Lauren's story, *Formal Arrangement*, book 4 in the Happy Endings Book Club series. Join the club and get your happy ending!

Formal Arrangement

Lauren Bishop has her whole summer planned out—working as a nanny for a desperate single dad and finding the elusive Mr. Right. She even signed up for the local match-making guru's Make Love Bloom (TM) service, end of summer guarantee! But somehow her plans got derailed because now she finds herself longing for her emotionally unavailable employer.

When his two-year-old's molars turn his little sunshine into a demon from hell, single dad Alex Campbell finds himself longing for the simpler days of teddy bear picnics. This is a parenting nightmare! Then sweet Lauren drops into their life like an angel sent from above. Alex doesn't do relationships, which is why he turns down every woman who comes his way, but he can't afford to lose this nanny. Can he convince her to stay even though she's looking for the one thing he can't give her?

Sign up for my newsletter and never miss a new release! kyliegilmore.com/newsletter

ALSO BY KYLIE GILMORE

Unleashed Romance <<steamy romcoms with dogs!

Fetching (Book 1)

Dashing (Book 2)

Sporting (Book 3)

Toying (Book 4)

Blazing (Book 5)

Chasing (Book 6)

Daring (Book 7)

Leading (Book 8)

Racing (Book 9)

Loving (Book 10)

The Clover Park Series <<brothers who put family first!

The Opposite of Wild (Book 1)

Daisy Does It All (Book 2)

Bad Taste in Men (Book 3)

Kissing Santa (Book 4)

Restless Harmony (Book 5)

Not My Romeo (Book 6)

Rev Me Up (Book 7)

An Ambitious Engagement (Book 8)

Clutch Player (Book 9)

A Tempting Friendship (Book 10)

Clover Park Bride: Nico and Lily's Wedding

A Valentine's Day Gift (Book 11)

Maggie Meets Her Match (Book 12)

The Clover Park STUDS series <<hawt geeks who unleash into studs!

Almost Over It (Book 1)

Almost Married (Book 2)

Almost Fate (Book 3)

Almost in Love (Book 4)

Almost Romance (Book 5)

Almost Hitched (Book 6)

Happy Endings Book Club Series <<the Campbell family and a romance book club collide!

Hidden Hollywood (Book 1)

Inviting Trouble (Book 2)

So Revealing (Book 3)

Formal Arrangement (Book 4)

Bad Boy Done Wrong (Book 5)

Mess With Me (Book 6)

Resisting Fate (Book 7)

Chance of Romance (Book 8)

Wicked Flirt (Book 9)

An Inconvenient Plan (Book 10)

A Happy Endings Wedding (Book 11)

The Rourkes Series <<swoonworthy princes and kickass princesses!

Royal Catch (Book 1)

Royal Hottie (Book 2)

Royal Darling (Book 3)

Royal Charmer (Book 4)

Royal Player (Book 5)

Royal Shark (Book 6)

Rogue Prince (Book 7)

Rogue Gentleman (Book 8)

Rogue Rascal (Book 9)

Rogue Angel (Book 10)

Rogue Devil (Book 11)

Rogue Beast (Book 12)

Check out my website for the most up-to-date list of my books:
kyliegilmore.com/books

ABOUT THE AUTHOR

Kylie Gilmore is the *USA Today* bestselling author of the Unleashed Romance series, the Rourkes series, the Happy Endings Book Club series, the Clover Park series, and the Clover Park STUDS series. She writes humorous romance that makes you laugh, cry, and reach for a cold glass of water.

Kylie lives in New York with her family, two cats, and a nutso dog. When she's not writing, reading hot romance, or dutifully taking notes at writing conferences, you can find her flexing her muscles all the way to the high cabinet for her secret chocolate stash.

Sign up for Kylie's Newsletter and get a FREE book! kyliegilmore.com/newsletter

For text alerts on Kylie's new releases, text KYLIE to the number (888) 707-3025. (US only)

For more fun stuff check out Kylie's website https://www.kyliegilmore.com.

Thanks for reading *So Revealing.* I hope you enjoyed it. Would you like to know about new releases? You can sign up for my new release email list at kyliegilmore.com/newsletter. I promise not to clog your inbox! Only new release info, sales, and some fun giveaways.

I love to hear from readers! You can find me at:
kyliegilmore.com
Instagram.com/kyliegilmore
Facebook.com/KylieGilmoreToo
Twitter @KylieGilmoreToo

If you liked Ty and Charlotte's story, please leave a review on your favorite retailer's website or Goodreads. Thank you.

www.ingramcontent.com/pod-product-compliance
Lightning Source LLC
Chambersburg PA
CBHW060750210726
48292CB00014B/2680